It was murder — and my parents were the victims. And I wasn't even allowed to see them, to hold them, to say . . . I don't know what I wanted to say. I just wanted to see them, because I suppose I didn't really believe that they could be dead. It seemed that if I actually saw them and touched them, could just be in the same room as them, then I'd see they were alive really. This was all an elaborate game of murder in the dark. See, here were the detectives . . . Turn on the lights, open the door. Let me in! Let me in! Let me in, you bastards! Let me in!

But they didn't, and I never saw my parents again — not even to identify the bodies, because my uncle did that. Someone responsible and capable and grown-up. An adult. I don't like adults. That's why I'm here, in this place. Though, God knows, there's enough of the bastards here.

Also by Alan Durant and available
in Definitions:

Flesh and Bones

Blood

ALAN DURANT

DEFINITIONS
in association with The Bodley Head

BLOOD
A DEFINITIONS BOOK 978 1 862 30437 6

First published in Great Britain by The Bodley Head,
an imprint of Random House Children's Books
A Random House Group Company

The Bodley Head edition published 1992
Red Fox edition published 1993
Definitions edition published 2007

3 5 7 9 10 8 6 4 2

The Random House Group Limited makes every effort to ensure that the papers used
in its books are made from trees that have been legally sourced from well-managed
and credibly certified forests. Our paper procurement policy can be found at:
www.randomhouse.co.uk/paper.htm

The Random House Group Limited supports The Forest Stewardship
Council (FSC®), the leading international forest certification organisation.
Our books carrying the FSC label are printed on FSC® certified paper.
FSC is the only forest certification scheme endorsed by the leading
environmental organisations, including Greenpeace. Our
paper procurement policy can be found at
www.randomhouse.co.uk/environment

Printed and bound in Great Britain by Clays Ltd, St Ives PLC

www.kidsatrandomhouse.co.uk
www.rbooks.co.uk

Addresses for companies within The Random House Group Limited can be found at:
www.randomhouse.co.uk/offices.htm

THE RANDOM HOUSE GROUP Limited Reg. No. 954009

A CIP catalogue record for this book is available from the British Library.

Printed in the UK by CPI Bookmarque, Croydon, CR0 4TD

For Ma and Dad
with love and thanks

The thing that really drove me crazy was that they wouldn't even let me see my own parents. When I came to the house – my house, me and my family's house – they wouldn't let me in. They said they couldn't let any-body in, because of disturbing the evidence and all that. But that was just a lot of crap. They didn't want me to see. I suppose they thought they were being very noble and protecting my poor juvenile feelings, but in fact they were messing up my feelings totally for ever. It wasn't all their fault, I suppose – they were just being adults. I don't ever want to be an adult.

Mr Lees, the headmaster, told me the news. I was in the middle of a homework detention with Vanissart, the Old Fart, when Mrs Bell, the school secretary, came in, looking embarrassed like she always did. She handed the Old Fart a note and he read it. Then he looked up with this serious expression on his face. The expression he had when he was about to deliver one of his pompous lectures. But this time he didn't give any lecture. He just looked at me and said, 'Harrison, you're to go to the headmaster's office. Now.' And so I did, thinking, What the hell have I done? What could I have done? I was thinking about whether I'd been late too many times the previous term, if someone had noticed I'd done a bunk one afternoon earlier in the week, if I was going to get a lecture about my GCSE results . . .

But it wasn't anything like that. I hadn't done anything. It had been done to me. Parenticide or whatever they call it. Only Lees didn't say that, of course. I don't even remember exactly what it was he said. He didn't say, 'Oh, Harrison, I'm sorry but your parents have just both been shot to death.' He didn't say, 'Sorry, Harrison, but you're now officially an orphan.' He didn't say, 'I'm afraid someone's just totally destroyed your life.' But he might just as well have done. Because that, basically, is what had happened.

There were police cars all over the place. Radios blurting out incomprehensible messages, lights flashing. The works. It was very weird, because the only time there were ever that many cars around the house, and all that noise, was when my parents were having one of their parties, and for a moment that was the thought that came into my head. But this was no party . . . It was murder – and my parents were the victims. And I wasn't even allowed to see them, to hold them, to say . . . I don't know what I wanted to say. I just wanted to see them, because I suppose I didn't really believe that they could be dead. It seemed that if I actually saw them and touched them, could just be in the same room as them, then I'd see they were alive really. This was all an elaborate game of murder in the dark. See, here were the detectives . . . Turn on the lights, open the door. Let me in! Let me in! Let me in, you bastards! Let me in!

But they didn't, and I never saw my parents again – not even to identify the bodies, because my uncle did that. Someone responsible and capable and grown-up. An adult. I don't like adults. That's why I'm here, in this place. Though, God knows, there's enough of the bastards here.

They never tell me the truth. I guess they're just incapable of it. Teachers, doctors, police, your own family even . . . I wasn't allowed into my own house, I wasn't allowed to see my own parents, but what do I see next day in the raggiest rag of the gutter press but a photograph of the whole bloody scene. The photograph was so badly printed that I didn't even realize what it was at first. What drew my attention to the photograph initially was this picture on the wall – it's a framed print of a painting entitled *La Lezione di Geografia* by a Venetian painter called Pietro Longhi – because I knew we had that picture up in our sitting room. It was my dad's favourite painting – he always used to say it was a very civilized picture, 'the encapsulation of a golden age'. There's a woman sitting down at a small table with a globe and a man standing with one hand in his jacket like Nelson, and the other hand holding one of those eyeglass things they used to have. He's peering through it at the globe – or the woman maybe. At the front on the left is a stout man dressed in brown, holding an atlas, and there's another atlas open at his feet. Above him there are shelves of huge books and a velvet drape. In the background another woman – a maid perhaps – is bringing a tray of coffee or tea. It looks like they're planning a great voyage. It's a wonderful painting. I've never seen it up anywhere else except on our wall. And I was on the verge of thinking, How strange that someone else should have that same painting, when of course I realized it was our sitting room and those were my father's old leather-bound volumes of Sir Walter Scott that were strewn about the floor and his whisky decanter that had smashed and stained the cream carpet and my mother's brains that had caused that thick, dark smear up the wall . . .

You couldn't have seen the faces very well even if there had been much to see. They were just figures slumped on the floor. Although, if you looked really closely, you could just about make out that the top half of my mother's skull was no longer there. But at least my father's face was turned away from the camera. He'd only been shot once – but the bullet had hit his heart. The doctor said they'd both died instantaneously, but then he knew that's what I wanted to hear, didn't he?

The headline read, SLAUGHTER IN SUBURBS! Then underneath it said: Thieves Murder Couple in Cold Blood. Then there was another line underneath: 'Catch these animals!' brother pleads. That's my mother's brother, Uncle Jim. What he actually said – not that it really matters – was that he wouldn't be able to sleep easy at nights until the killers were brought to justice. But that sort of talk doesn't sell newspapers. Murder, rape, assault, mutilation, child abuse, torture, threats – violence in all its vile shapes and sizes – that's what sells newspapers, isn't it? Well, there was plenty of evidence of it in that wrecked and bloody room, from whose blood-spattered walls an elegant Venetian peered through his eyeglass at the carnage beneath him as if to say, 'What on earth has become of this great wonderful civilized world of ours?'

I was travelling on a bus at the time. God knows why. I was still in a state of shock and certainly not fit to be out in public. But I was staying at my uncle's and suddenly I needed some air. I had to get out. When I saw the photograph and the headlines, well, then I flipped. I snatched the paper from the guy sitting in front of me and I started to rip it apart – tear it into shreds. He started shouting and then I just went hysterical . . . I don't remember much after that. Apparently – so Aunty Susan says – some young guy and his girlfriend helped get me home. For some days after that I was in a pretty bad state and didn't see anyone and then it was the funeral.

And I don't want to talk about that.

Old Sigmund's just finished reading what I wrote in the notebook about Mum and Dad's death, and he gave me another one of his bloody lectures – sorry, very reasonable arguments. (I suppose I should introduce Sigmund – for posterity's sake. His real name is Dr Ackfield. He's a shrink in this place they sent me to. I call him Sigmund because I want to annoy him.)

Anyway, what Sigmund said is that I should go back to the beginning of this whole sordid business and relive what was happening to me at the time. He wants me to put down in his poxy notebook what I felt then, not in retrospect – i.e. he wants me to cut out all the rude bits about doctors and police and adults in general. I said, 'What you mean is, you want me to be selective with the truth.' And he said no, he wanted the whole truth – had to have it, in order to help me – but he wanted the pure truth, not my subsequent interpretation of it. And I said, 'How can I just forget what I've learned?' And he said that he agreed I couldn't, not entirely, but he thought I should try. Not *must* try, you notice – he's far too reasonable for that. But *should* try. Well, sod him, because if he thinks I'm going to write down all that stuff about the funeral just so that he can get a kick out of my grief, he can think again. If there's something I don't want to talk about, then I won't. That's my right, and I think I've bloody well earned it after all I've been through . . .

I'd just started my first term in the sixth form when it happened. But I didn't go back. For a few weeks I didn't really do anything at all. Those weeks seemed to last for ever, as though time had just stopped – like a tide that had gone out for good and left me washed up and stranded. I lay upstairs in my adopted bedroom most of the time, where no one could see me. Where I could be alone with my misery and my memories, spaced out on sedatives. Doctors, psychiatric nurses, counsellors of one sort or another came and went and made various therapeutic suggestions – but I didn't take anything in. Just about the only thing I could communicate with was the bare, painted walls and ceiling of my room. I'd stare at the cracks in the ceiling for hours on end, tracing their jagged lines back and forth, back and forth, thinking about nothing in particular. It was like I was there but didn't really exist.

I hardly spoke to Uncle Jim or Aunty Susan at all. Yet,

for as long as I could remember, Uncle Jim had been like a second father to me. Sometimes he even seemed more like my father than my real father, Dad was away so much. Dad was export sales director for a multinational aluminium company. He was always flying off around the world somewhere or other to sell his company's products – foil mainly. Whenever he introduced Dad to anyone, Uncle Jim always used to say: 'This is David. He's in foil.' It never failed to make someone laugh. It always made me laugh – not so much at the joke, but at the way people responded. I remember one summer at a family party, Uncle Jim introducing Dad to a very old and distant relative of Aunty Susan's who'd just come back from Singapore or somewhere. Uncle Jim said his usual line. The old woman leant forward, took hold of Dad's arm and said very seriously: 'You poor man, you must be baking.' I laughed a lot at that. Everyone did.

It was Uncle Jim who taught me how to ride a bike; Uncle Jim who took me to my first football match and explained the rules; Uncle Jim who showed me how to fire an air pistol . . . But not even he could teach me how to live without my parents. I couldn't talk to him, and he couldn't get through to me – no matter how hard he tried. A real tension developed between us.

'You've got to start thinking of the future, Robert,' he said one dinner time, when the three of us sat glumly round the kitchen table, like strangers in a station buffet. I knew what he was driving at because he'd mentioned it long before all this terrible stuff had happened; he wanted me to go into his company. Uncle Jim was a pretty big fish in our small pond – he had a thriving central heating and boiler business, as well as being a prominent local councillor with aspirations towards one day being mayor. I couldn't see what possible use I could be to him.

'You can't just sit in that room moping for ever,' he said.

'Why not?' I replied. 'Why shouldn't I just sit there? What's the point of doing anything?'

'You've got a life to live,' he said. 'You owe it to your parents. You owe it to yourself.'

'My parents are dead,' I said, bitterly. 'I don't owe anyone anything. Just leave me alone.'

And that was the end of another depressing meal. I stormed out and went back up to my room – or 'tomb' as Uncle Jim had once, in a moment of frustration, referred to it.

It went on like that for weeks. And then one day I decided that I just had to get out. I felt like I was being suffocated in that house, under the weight of Uncle Jim and Aunty Susan's concern, and I knew that they must be finding living with me pretty unbearable. I decided it was time I went home – just for a few days. I thought it might help to lessen the sense of rootlessness that I was feeling. It *was* my home after all, despite what had happened. All my stuff was there – my clothes, my books, my music . . .

I knew Uncle Jim and Aunty Susan would object if I told them face to face what I wanted to do – and I didn't want to get into a row. So I wrote them a note, explaining how I was feeling and that it would only be for a day or so and that they didn't have to worry about me doing anything stupid. (I think they knew that anyway – I'd gone through the suicidal stage.) I waited until they'd both gone out, packed my bags, left the note, and went back home.

The first thing that struck me when I got off the bus was the smell. It was that distinctive, pungent, smoky, sort of melancholy smell that is the hallmark of autumn in the suburbs. Sundays in particular. It immediately evoked pictures of Sunday morning walks, collecting conkers, my father burning leaves in the garden, arriving home from school to a warm house and my mother's smiling face . . . Cosy family scenes that would now only live in photograph albums and my memory. My poor bloodstained memory.

My parents' house was at the end of a cul-de-sac, some distance from the other houses in the road and further cut off by a tall hedge and a long driveway. Two months had passed since I'd last been here. Then it had been late summer and the place had been teeming with police cars and activity. Now it was as quiet as . . . well, as quiet as the grave. Everything was brown and barren-looking. Walking through the gateway was like walking into a cemetery. The garden was buried under fallen leaves. The house looked like it had been empty for years rather than just a couple of months. I shivered. It was weird, disquieting, how quickly the familiar had become strange. I felt as though the I who was now walking up the drive was not the same I who had lived here for over seventeen years. I felt like a stranger, an intruder. I felt uncomfortable being alive.

That first night back was the worst. I walked around the house, pacing from room to room, but not daring to go into *the* room – the room where it had all happened. I was scared, horrified about what I might see. What if they hadn't cleared up all the mess? What if blood still stained the walls and carpet? What if – it was crazy, but I couldn't get it out of my mind – my parents' bloody, dehumanized corpses were still there? But, behind it all, what was really terrible, I suppose, was the knowledge that they wouldn't be there. Not now. Not ever.

I knew I'd have to go into the sitting room eventually, though. I couldn't avoid it for ever. After all, it was the last place Mum and Dad had been alive. But it was hard going through the door. It made me shake violently for a moment . . . I looked around. The room had been meticulously tidied. Put back to normal, I suppose 'they' would have said – that is, whoever had done the tidying. Only it was actually much too clinically tidy to be normal. Mum was always very particular about keeping the place clean and orderly, but her tidiness wasn't like most people's – it was sort of haphazard. A kind of ordered chaos rather than neatness. Dad was quite different; he tended to put things anywhere. It was one of the things that drove Mum crazy. Now everything (everything that was left, that is) was sort of in its rightful place, but arranged in a completely foreign way.

There was a faint smudge (which I thought might have been blood) on the paintwork by the door, just where my mother had been shot, but apart from that you'd never have known that this room had recently been the scene of a brutal, bloody murder. Someone had even carefully cleaned up Dad's leather-bound volumes of Sir Walter Scott and put them back on the bookshelves in order. They stood alongside the many other old, impressive, but mainly unread tomes that Dad had collected over the years. Dad was a great collector, but not a great reader. It was the same with music. He had lots of records and could tell you why this version of Mahler's Sixth was superior to that version. But he wasn't really an avid listener – he just read an awful lot of LP covers. He collected stamps too. But I think that probably had something to do with all the travelling he did. It was a way of collecting places.

Dad had been just about everywhere. Hardly a month went by than he was off somewhere or other. Maybe that's why he loved that painting by Longhi so much. France (his favourite place), Germany, Holland, Scandinavia, Russia, India, Thailand, Japan, Lebanon, the USA . . . you name it, he'd been there – and brought back souvenirs to prove it: T-shirts, scarves, jewellery, knick-knacks, and lots of food (wrapped in foil, of course). The sitting room was full of such souvenirs – an ashtray from the Raffles Hotel in Singapore, a series of blue commemorative plates from Copenhagen (two of which were now badly cracked), a small white elephant, carved in ivory, from somewhere in Africa . . .

He once nearly died of food poisoning in Iraq and had a close shave with the Tontons Macoute in Haiti; he slept in hotel rooms with rats and snakes and one time shared a bed with a scorpion; he saw many wonderful things and many terrible things – and in the end he was murdered at home, in his own sitting room, in the suburbs, in civilized, boring old England. And it had happened in this room, where I was standing, wondering why it had happened, why it had had to happen to him, to them, to us . . .

* * *

I stayed in that room all night. Uncle Jim phoned in the evening to see that I was OK and I told him I was and just needed some time on my own – and he seemed to understand. Then I got a sleeping bag from the airing cupboard and took it down to the sitting room and slept there, on the sofa, because I thought somehow it might help me to get near Mum and Dad. I hardly slept at all, but when I did I dreamt that Mum and I were out in the country somewhere, waiting for Dad. We were very happy and laughed a lot. Dad was going to arrive soon and then we were all going to go off together to another country where, Mum said, we could pick wild strawberries off the trees. And I laughed and said 'Great', but I started to feel uneasy and Dad didn't turn up. Then a bell started ringing, which meant Dad's flight was about to come in (we were at the airport now) – but he never arrived, because I woke up.

The bell went on ringing. I opened my eyes to darkness and for a few moments had no idea where I was. Then I remembered and my mind registered that the telephone was ringing. It brought me back to reality with a real crash. I felt so depressed I just wanted to pull the sleeping bag up over my head, like one of those body-bag things they send dead soldiers home in, to try and shut out everything. But the ringing didn't stop. And, in the end, I realized that the only way I'd ever make it stop would be to answer it.

I was expecting it to be Uncle Jim again, but I didn't recognize the voice on the other end of the line. Whoever it was knew my name, though, and seemed to be asking me how I was. I was puzzled, wondering who on earth could know I was there. Then the voice identified itself. It belonged to a work colleague of Dad's, Gerald Finch. I'd met him once or twice, briefly. I supposed Uncle Jim must have told him I was at home. He wanted to know if I'd like to have lunch with him. He said he thought I might like to talk about Dad to someone. Or just get out. He had a few things to discuss too – but only if I felt up to it. Nothing important. I didn't really feel like seeing anyone, but, in my half-asleep state, the prospect of getting out of the house, getting away from everything for a while, suddenly seemed appealing. So I said yes. He said he'd send a car to collect me around noon. Then hung up.

Almost at once, the phone rang again. It was a Detective Chief Inspector Donnelly of New Scotland Yard. He wondered if I felt up to answering a few questions and if he could come round. I ought to have told him to get stuffed, the way the police had treated me, but I was too surprised to say anything. I'd only been back home for one night and already everyone seemed to know I was there. Donnelly evidently took my silence as a 'yes', because he said he'd be round at eleven. Then he rang off.

Chief Inspector Donnelly was as good as his word. The elegant Viennese regulator clock in the hallway (actually not Viennese at all, but a souvenir from Germany) was still chiming the hour when the doorbell rang. I opened the door to bright sunshine. I hadn't yet opened the curtains, and this first glare of sunlight dazzled me. I could hardly see the tall man standing on the doorstep.

'Good morning, sir,' he said. 'Detective Chief Inspector Donnelly.'

'Come in,' I said, anxious to get away from the blinding light.

He followed me through to the gloomy sitting room.

'I hope I didn't get you up,' he said, looking at the crumpled sleeping bag and the closed curtains.

'This is where I slept,' I said.

It sounded stupid, but I couldn't think of anything else to say. I couldn't explain *why* I'd slept there to a policeman. Not even if I'd wanted to. I'd have felt embarrassed trying to explain it to anyone. To cover my discomfort I busied myself with gathering up the sleeping bag.

'I won't keep you long,' Donnelly said. 'May I sit down?'

Chief Inspector Donnelly seemed even bigger sitting

down than he had standing up. Dad was pretty tall – over six feet – and I was no midget myself, but when Donnelly sat down in Dad's favourite armchair, he made it look like it was a model made to a smaller scale than the real thing. He tried to sit straight, but it was very difficult in that chair because the seat tipped back quite a lot where the upholstery was broken. He tried to compensate by tilting his large square head forward. He didn't look at all comfortable, but he also looked like someone who was used to not being comfortable. Suddenly the room seemed very full.

'We haven't met before, have we?' he began, pulling at the creases in his trousers with his big hands. For a large man, he had a surprisingly small voice – a bit thin and strained. The sort of voice that made you want to cough and clear your throat.

I shook my head.

'After the' – he hesitated a moment, trying to find the right word. The word that wouldn't offend. The neutral word: polispeak – 'incident, I believe you had an interview with Detective Sergeant Barnes.'

I nodded. It hadn't been a very pleasant experience. Detective Sergeant Barnes was one of those policemen I'd often heard about on post-party Mondays at school – a bully with a sledgehammer approach. His method of asking questions was to shout and swear a lot. Well, I shouted and swore a lot too. So we didn't get very far. Mind you, I was feeling so angry and hysterical at the time that I probably would have bawled out Mother Teresa. But I didn't see why he had to ask all that personal stuff about Mum, Dad and me. It was family business, not his – it didn't have anything to do with the murders. In the end, Uncle Jim stepped in and put a stop to the questioning. He was very good about that. God knows what would have happened if he hadn't been around. ~~But then~~

'Detective Sergeant Barnes's approach leaves a little to be desired,' Donnelly continued. He paused for a moment as if he were going to expand on this statement. But he didn't. Instead he pursed his lips and rubbed his bristly, greying moustache. Then he smiled briefly.

'Mr Mowbray, your uncle, has been of great assistance in our investigation – except in the matter of letting us speak to you, of course . . .' He paused again, pulling once more at the creases in his trousers. 'He has very kindly helped us compile a list of items believed stolen in the robbery. Obviously, though, you would have a better knowledge than he of what was in the house before the robbery and what is now missing. So, I wonder if you would mind casting your eyes over this' – he reached into his pocket and took out a piece of paper – 'and seeing if there's anything that should be added.'

I took the piece of paper.

'So the motive was robbery, was it?' I said.

It suddenly dawned on me how little I knew about what had happened. I knew my parents had been murdered – and how. I'd seen the pictures. But that was about it. I hadn't been able – or wanted – to talk about it to anyone. Not even Uncle Jim. But then I'd hardly spoken to or seen anyone for two months, lying in my room, sedated up to the eyeballs.

'It would appear so,' said Donnelly. 'But I'm afraid that, as yet, we've made very little progress in tracing the villains.'

Villains, I thought. Another piece of polispeak. The sort of word you might use to describe a group of conmen or kids who nick the radios out of cars. In relation to the enormity of this crime, it seemed absurdly inadequate. Cold-blooded murderers, vile monsters, inhuman bastards . . . surely that's what we were dealing with here. Not 'villains'.

I looked at the typewritten list in my hands. No doubt to whoever had typed this list, to Donnelly and any other policeman who'd read it, it was just another catalogue of stolen items. Another list of possible clues. To me, though, every object was part of a family scene or scenes. Scenes that would never ever be repeated. Every object evoked memories that made my throat tighten.

'Is there anything missing from the list?' asked Donnelly.

'I don't think so,' I said. 'But I couldn't say for sure until I've had a proper look around. I only came back yesterday.'

'Of course, of course,' he said. 'Well, if you could have a look around over the next couple of days and let me know if you find anything – or, rather, don't find anything – I would be most grateful.'

I nodded.

Donnelly got up. He walked over to the bookshelf and picked up a 'vase' full of dried flowers. The vase was actually a grotesque jug, fashioned in the shape of a bird with blue and green wings and with massive talons and beak. It was one of my father's favourite objects – and one of my mother's least favourite. In fact, she only agreed to let it stay in the sitting room on condition that it was masked with flowers. Donnelly held up the heavy object, as though it were a piece of balsa wood.

'Your parents were very keen collectors, son, weren't they?'

'My mother was,' I said. 'My father travelled a lot. He always brought things back with him.'

'Very valuable things too,' he said, 'some of them. Like this' – he paused again, uncertain just how to describe the peculiar object in his hand – 'this bird, for instance. I saw one of these before on a television programme a few years back. *Antiques Roadshow*. So I thought I'd have it valued. It might interest you to learn – if you don't know already – that this bird was made in 1906 by the Martin brothers and is currently worth something in the region of five thousand pounds.'

I looked at him, amazed.

'Five thousand pounds!' I said.

'Yes,' he said. 'There's no accounting for taste, is there? Anyway, that's one of the strange things about this case. You see, we believe that whoever was responsible for the robbery and murder of your parents was professional. They took objects of value – collector's items and jewellery. They left no fingerprints and no clues. And yet they left this.' He looked at the jug with a puzzled frown. 'One of the most valuable items that was in the room at the time.' He gave a small shake of his large head and put the jug back on the bookshelf.

I didn't say anything. I just looked at the jug with astonishment. I was used to it being a source of friction and/or amusement; it seemed incredible that it was actually valuable. My mother used to refer to it as 'that ghastly bird'; my father said it reminded him of someone he knew and that he found it very funny; I always thought it looked like the caricature of a stern Dickensian schoolmaster.

Donnelly had walked over to the window.

'Do you mind if I draw back the curtains, son?' he asked. 'Let in a bit of daylight.'

'No,' I said. 'I mean, draw them back if you want. I don't really care.'

He drew them back and suddenly the room was full of daylight, although my head was still full of night.

'Tell me, Robert,' Donnelly said, using my Christian name for the first time, as though letting in the sunlight was the signal for an increase in familiarity, 'was it usual for your father to be at home in the afternoon?'

'No,' I said, 'not unless he'd just come back from a trip, or was about to go on one.'

'I see. And was that the case on the afternoon of the shooting?'

I thought for a moment – and was a little taken aback to realize I didn't know the answer.

'I don't know,' I said. 'Dad hadn't just come back from anywhere, so I suppose he must have been going away. I don't know where to though. He often went away without any notice. To me, I mean. You'd have to ask at UKA, where he worked.'

'We already have,' said Donnelly. 'I just thought you might be able to shed a little more light on the matter.' He smoothed his moustache contemplatively. 'And what about your mother?' he asked. 'Did she accompany your father on his trips?'

'No,' I said. 'She had a job of her own. She worked mornings at the local antiques shop.'

'I see,' said Donnelly thoughtfully.

He turned away and looked out through the windows into the garden and beyond to where his car was parked in the street. For a moment or two he stood in silence. Then he said, 'Tell me, Robert, did you by any chance see anything or anyone at all suspicious during the week or so previous to the murders? An unexpected caller perhaps, or someone lurking in the street.'

I tried to think back to the week before it had happened, but nothing came. All I could think of was the awful day itself, the photograph in the newspaper, the funeral . . . Even the day before it happened seemed like a lifetime ago. Two lifetimes ago. I had an uncomfortable feeling that at any moment I was going to start crying.

'Well,' said Donnelly, 'if you do recall anything I'd be grateful if you'd contact me at the Yard.'

I nodded my head. Donnelly started to do up his coat. I think he sensed my distress.

'Listen, son,' he said, when his coat was finally buttoned. 'If you'll take my advice, you'll go back and stay with your uncle. You'll be better off there – and safer. This is no place for a young lad to be staying on his own . . . Go back to the world of the living.'

Donnelly's curiously paternal tone had a very different effect from the one I think he'd intended. Instead of softening me up, it made me pull myself together. All of a sudden I felt harder, tougher. I was independent now, my own man, and I wasn't going to let anyone tell me what to do. I no longer felt like crying – I felt like demanding. I wasn't going to let Donnelly treat me like some soppy kid. So I made the toughest demand of all. The demand that would take the lid off the whole horrible can of worms. The question I hadn't thought I'd dare ask.

'Before you go, Chief Inspector,' I said, 'I want to know . . . I want you to tell me what really happened.'

He didn't want to tell me. He tried to evade the issue by saying they couldn't be certain and it was all speculation et cetera. But in the end I made him tell me. It was my right to know – and he knew it. So he told me.

The murderer or murderers (Donnelly suspected it had been the work of a gang) arrived at the house at some time between two (when Mum generally got home from work) and three. There were no windows forced or broken and the burglar alarm hadn't been tampered with, so Donnelly's conclusion was that the thieves had come through the front door. They'd probably posed as workmen of some sort – telephone engineers or men from the gas board – and gained entry that way. It wouldn't have taken that much to convince Mum, I thought. She was always opening the front door to complete strangers. Maybe it was because Dad was away so much that she did so many things that men do, but women aren't supposed to. Like opening her front door without enquiring first who was there, just because someone knocked on it. Well, once the thieves got inside they held her at gunpoint – one of them holding a gun to her head – and started robbing the place. Donnelly reckoned (only speculation, he stressed) that Dad probably arrived and disturbed them while this was going on and that might have been what caused the shooting. Maybe he tried to tackle them and one of them shot him. Then the one holding a gun to Mum's head shot her too. After that the thieves took their loot and fled.

'And that was that,' I said bitterly.

'Well,' said Donnelly, 'not quite. At 3.37 p.m. the local police station received a call informing them that there had been a fatal accident at this address. The caller identified himself only as "a neighbour". We have, of course, questioned all of the people in the immediate area and, needless to say, none of them made that call.'

'Sounds like the bastards had a very sick sense of humour,' I said. I was starting to feel very sick myself. It had suddenly come home to me how near to death I myself had been that afternoon. Supposing I'd bunked off the last lesson and gone home early as I'd done often enough in the past. I might have walked right into it . . .

'Well,' said Donnelly, 'whatever the reason, it's a very curious occurrence and that is not at all a bad thing. You'd be amazed how often curious occurrences turn out to be the crucial element in solving a crime. It gives us a bit of hope anyway.'

Donnelly's final remark resonated in my head for some time after he'd gone. I wasn't quite sure whether it was said to reassure me or himself. If it was meant for me, he might just as well have saved his breath, because hope was the one thing I had nothing of. Not even a little bit. What on earth did I have to hope for? His hope seemed nothing more than a bolted stable door. He hoped to bring the criminals to justice. But those very same criminals had killed my hope a couple of months ago and catching them wasn't going to bring it – or my parents – back again.

I went out to the kitchen and sat at the table while I waited for the car Gerald Finch was sending. I had another look at the list of stolen items Donnelly had given me. The most valuable object was the blue Chinese Ming bowl that Mum had inherited from her grandmother years ago and which had really started her passion for collecting. It had stood in a glass display case, all on its own, like a museum exhibit, opposite the door, so that no one who went into the sitting room could help noticing and being impressed by it. Then there was the lavish and intricate red and gold nineteenth-century chess set from Madras (my favourite object) which Dad taught me to play chess on – much to Mum's displeasure; she thought it much too fine to actually play with. But we played with it all the same. I used to play with it for hours on my own when Mum wasn't around – not working out chess gambits, but arranging the opposing armies, complete with elephants and retainers, so that the board took on wonderful, vividly coloured patterns.

Next on the list were Mum's Staffordshire pottery figures and the collection of thimbles from Meissen in Germany that Dad had bought her. I remember when he gave her the first one. I was about seven at the time and thought a thimble just about the most boring birthday present imaginable. Much to my surprise though, Mum was delighted. I can still recall the radiant smile that lit up her face and the joyful way she swept back her blonde hair. She always did that when she received a pleasant and unexpected surprise. It was a gesture I loved, because it meant she was in a good mood.

The last time I'd seen her make that gesture had been nine weeks ago – on the morning of her murder. I'd been sitting at this very table, eating my breakfast before my usual mad rush to school, while she pottered about the kitchen, making coffee, watering her plants, listening to the news on Radio Four. There had been an item about GCSE exam results – which was a bit of a taboo subject in our house, considering the hash I'd made of my exams the previous summer. I was busily eating my cornflakes, trying to ignore the radio, when some educational expert came on the air. He said that although results had in general been better than ever before, there was one subject which had shown a marked drop in standards – geography . . . which just happened to be the one and only subject I had excelled at. I looked up from my breakfast and caught Mum's eye as she glanced across at me. We both grinned and Mum put her hand on her forehead and threw back her hair. 'You needn't look quite so smug,' she said, smiling. 'One swallow doesn't make a summer, you know.'

Then she hurried me off to school. I didn't even get a chance to wash up my bowl and spoon. She must have done it when I'd gone. It was still there, in the rack by the sink, where she'd put it to dry, all those days ago. It was like time had just stood still and any moment she might come through the door and start talking to me. Just for an instant I almost believed she would. I had such a strong picture of her.

I looked down again at the list. As I did, a tear dropped from my face on to the paper. And then the whole thing became a blur. My body shook with sobs. I put my head back and wept — like at the funeral. Tears for them, tears for me. Desolate, hopeless tears for all those times we had that led to nothing at all and wouldn't ever come again . . .

That's it. I'm not writing any more. Sigmund, you can go to hell — or wherever it is bastard shrinks go to when they've finished their tormenting down here on earth. And you can take all of the other two-faced, double-dealing, bull-shitting adult bastards with you.

Would you believe it? Sigmund read what I wrote – all that stuff about the deaths and Donnelly and my grief – but did he ask me about any of it? No. He wanted to talk about my dream. The one I had that first night in the house. It hardly seemed to me to be the most significant aspect of my narrative, but then he's the doctor – even if he is a prying bastard. I decided I might as well humour him. Anything to get off the subject of my parents' deaths, I thought.

He asked me what the dream suggested to me. I said it suggested to me that I needed a holiday. Then he asked me about the wild strawberries. I said that I liked strawberries – was there anything so weird about that? He looked at me for a moment, with that cool, detached look of his, then he closed his book, put the top back on his pen, clipped it back into his inside pocket and kneaded his hands together on the desk in front of him. That was it for the day, he said.

'That's it?' I said incredulously. 'That's it! What do you mean, that's it? You make me sit in my room writing all that crap for you and then after two minutes of talking you say, That's it? What sort of treatment is this?'

He said it was very poor treatment – useless treatment, and always would be unless I was prepared to co-operate. He said he knew it wasn't easy and it would certainly get harder, but if I went along with it, then we had a good chance of sorting this problem out. Reliving my story, unravelling my dreams . . . It was difficult, even unpleasant work, but it needed doing, and if I wasn't prepared to do it, well, he couldn't help me. Some bloody lecture – but it got through. I had to admit he had a point. After all, I don't want to stay in this dreadful place for ever.

So, reluctantly, I co-operated. I told him what the various parts of the dream meant to me . . .

Mum loved the countryside and so did I. When Dad was away we often used to go for long walks together out in the country. Dad didn't like walking really. And he found the countryside dull.

'When you've seen one tree, you've seen them all,' he used to say. Or 'Give me a bloody great skyscraper any day.'

The bit about wild strawberries came from a news-paper article Dad found in some provincial American newspaper on one of his trips. In it, some professor claimed that the rise in the number of cases of insanity during the summer was caused by people eating wild strawberries. When Mum had one of her moods, Dad used to say she'd been eating too many wild strawberries again. It became a bit of a family joke. Also, of course, strawberries don't grow on trees – so no wonder I was feeling uneasy.

As for the journey bit, well, I may not be the world's greatest expert on dream symbolism, but there are two kinds of dream that I do know about. One is flying, which is supposed to be something to do with sex, and the other is travelling, which is a symbol for death. I guess I'd been feeling pretty suicidal the night of my dream and I just wanted to be reunited with my parents – even if it meant I had to die for it to happen.

Sigmund listened without saying a word. Every now and then he just nodded or made a note in his book. When I finished he thanked me. Then he asked me if there was anything else I wanted to add. I said that I couldn't think of anything.

'What do you think of my analysis, then?' I joked. 'Do you think I'll make a shrink one day?'

He said he doubted it, but it was very interesting all the same. Then he asked me about my parents. Did I get on with them? Did they get on with me? How did I feel about them – now and before?

Well, it was a bit like that Sergeant Barnes episode all over again. I got really angry. It was partly, I think, that I wasn't prepared for anything quite so direct and partly because the questions seemed insulting somehow, as if Sigmund were casting doubts on my love for my parents and theirs for me. It seemed sort of sacrilegious. I told Sigmund that if he were trying to make me feel guilty, then he could go to hell – I had nothing to feel guilty about. And that really was the end of that for the day.

Since then, though, I've done quite a bit of thinking about Sigmund's questions. And I've come to the conclusion that maybe there was something in them after all. I mean, it's funny, isn't it – your parents are the people you're closest to in the world, and yet somehow, when you really come to think about it, how well can you say you know them, as people? I would say that I got on with my parents pretty well and they got on pretty well with me, but I'm not sure that I could really say I knew them or exactly how they felt about me. Or even how I felt about them. They were my parents and I loved them. It was something I just never thought about.

I think I was a disappointment to them. Both of them. I don't think I lived up to their expectations. I was an only child so they put all their hopes in me. I was very bright when I was little – precocious. I spoke early and said lots of cute and clever things and everyone in the family thought I was some sort of prodigy. I went to school a year earlier than most kids and streaked ahead for the first few years. Great things were predicted for me. But then, gradually, I slowed down – or the rest caught up – and by the time I went to secondary school I was no longer out in front, but slipping down the pack, until I settled somewhere in the middle. I became Mister Average – not really outstanding at anything, except geography perhaps. I had few friends – and none close. I wasn't in the football eleven or the debating team. Even my interest in and ability at chess waned somewhere about the third year. When I only just managed to scrape into the sixth form, I think it was the final straw really. Certainly as far as Dad was concerned. I think he wrote me off as a duffer. I think that . . . I think . . . I think that now I won't ever have the chance to prove him wrong.

Gerald Finch's car arrived late, which gave me a bit of time to pull myself together. The chauffeur had the radio on and hardly said a word the whole journey – which suited me fine. By the time we got to London and the doors of the restaurant, I was feeling a lot more like myself – which is a pretty curious expression when you think about it. But in my case it was very apt: I'd been through so much over the last couple of months that a lot of the time I really didn't know just who I was.

The restaurant was a pretty flash West End place called Mario's. A waiter with a big smile, a very flamboyant walrus moustache and a dark suit met me at the door and showed me to my table. It was very crowded and just about everyone in the place was wearing a suit – even the women. I felt them watching me, in my jeans, sweater and Doc Martens, as I walked past. I hadn't thought about my clothes and whether they'd be suitable or not ... The last thing I wanted just now was to have everyone stare at me. That kind of attention is not something I've ever been very keen on.

The warmth of Gerald Finch's welcome made me feel a lot more comfortable. It didn't seem to bother him in the slightest what I was wearing.

'Ah, Robert,' he said, smiling and taking off the glasses he'd been wearing to look at the menu. 'How nice to see you again.'

He grasped my hand firmly for a moment.

'Sit down, sit down,' he said, gesturing towards the chair opposite his. 'Now, what would you like to drink? How about some wine? Do you drink wine?'

I nodded.

He turned to the waiter and spoke to him in Italian.

Gerald had a very warm smile. It complemented perfectly his manner on the telephone. When he asked me how I was and whether I needed anything – money or whatever – he really sounded like he meant it. I felt a bit embarrassed getting that much attention, but I appreciated it all the same. He said I could phone him any time – at work or home – if I needed anything or just wanted to talk. He gave me a card with his home number written on the back. It's probably still in my jeans pocket now.

Instead of the waiter Mario himself brought the wine and a silver bucket full of ice. He opened the bottle with a flourish and poured a little wine into Gerald's glass. Gerald lifted it and sniffed the wine delicately before tasting it. The way he did it reminded me of Dad. '*Molto buono, Mario,*' he said – or something like that. Dad always liked showing off his languages in restaurants too. Whereas I hate it – if I have to say anything foreign I always go red. Which is why I felt pretty uncomfortable now, when Mario got out a notepad and pen and prepared to take our order.

I looked hard at the menu – it was all in Italian. With great relief my eyes settled on the word minestrone and I ordered that. I sat back and took a gulp of my wine.

'And for ze main course?' asked Mario.

I looked at him vacantly, then I looked at the menu. For a moment it was like being back at school, in the first year, faced with a series of incomprehensible Latin exercises. Fortunately, Gerald came to my aid.

'What is the chef's special today, Mario?' he asked in English.

'Ah, Mr Finch,' said Mario with great relish, 'you weel love ze special today.'

Then he reeled off something in Italian. Gerald turned towards me.

'It's fish,' he said. 'Baked mackerel.'

I'm not a great fan of fish, either on or off the plate, but ordering the mackerel seemed the easiest option. So, mackerel it was.

'He's a great character,' said Gerald, when Mario had flounced off. 'And the food is quite excellent.'

I nodded and smiled. My face was starting to feel hot from the wine. Gerald refilled my glass and topped up his own.

'I used to come here a lot with your father,' he said. 'It was one of his favourite restaurants . . .'

He looked down for a moment, then he cleared his throat. When he looked up again, his face was sombre, the way old Vanissart's had been that day when he sent me to see the headmaster.

'I hope you don't mind talking about your father, Robert. If you do, just say and . . .'

I said it was OK. He nodded, then cleared his throat.

'He was very highly thought of in the company. Very much admired. He will be very sorely missed . . . I didn't know your mother that well – we only met a few times – but she was a very nice woman. It was a terrible, terrible tragedy. I really can't say how sorry we all are . . .'

While Gerald spoke, I watched his face, avoiding his eyes. I noticed the fascinating pattern of lines formed by his frown – two deep grooves on his forehead, two beneath his eyes and two by his mouth. For a moment, the rest of his features faded into the background. Then, when they came back into focus, they seemed that much more defined: the dark, deep-set eyes, the heavy eyebrows, the rather beaky nose . . . And then I realized just who it was that that Martinware bird jug of Dad's had reminded him of.

Gerald's frown deepened. He looked a little puzzled. Then I caught on that it must be my own expression that was the cause. Suddenly seeing Gerald as the Martinware bird had brought a smile to my face – my first real smile for weeks. It must have seemed to Gerald, though, like a pretty inappropriate response to what he'd just been saying.

'I was just thinking about Dad,' I said.

Gerald's face relaxed a little.

'I'm glad that you're able to remember him with a smile,' he said. 'I'm sure that's the way he would have wanted to be remembered. He was quite a joker, your father.'

Gerald took a piece of bread from the basket on the table and started to butter it.

A picture of Dad's smiling face came into my mind. Dad smiled a lot, but it was a tight, well-controlled smile – not open like Gerald's. It was an ironic, often sarcastic smile, like his sense of humour – very funny, as long as you weren't the butt of it, which increasingly over the last couple of years I had become. Mum too.

Our starters arrived. The soup smelt delicious. It was a couple of days since I'd had a proper meal and weeks since I'd had any kind of appetite. Today was the first time since the tragedy, and I couldn't help feeling – momentarily anyway – a bit guilty about it. In the end, though, my hunger overcame my qualms and I tucked in heartily.

Gerald ordered another bottle of wine.

'Do you know, Robert,' he said, taking a brief time-out from his spaghetti with clam sauce, 'the first time your father and I ever took a customer out to lunch together we came to this place? That must have been . . . oh . . . twelve years ago. Not long, in fact, after he joined the company. I'd only been with UKA a few months myself.' His heavy eyebrows formed into a V. 'It hardly seems like yesterday.'

I tried to remember what Dad had looked like in those days. Twelve years ago, he'd have been thirty-three. He'd have had more hair then; he was going quite bald now. No, he had been going quite bald . . . At one time, I remembered, he'd had a moustache. Mum hadn't liked it. I think it was because it made him look like some disreputable politician who was notorious at the time. But what time was it? The wine was starting to make thinking pretty difficult.

'Did Dad have a moustache in those days?' I asked.

Gerald looked at me, a little surprised. He thought for a moment.

'Yes,' he said. 'I believe he did. In fact, yes, of course he did. Because when he first joined, everyone used to say he looked like . . . What was that chap's name? Some politician who was in the news for . . . fraud, I think it was.' Gerald frowned again. Then his eyebrows levelled out once more.

'Your father was a terrific salesman,' he said. 'The best. I remember how impressed I was when I saw him in action that first time. He had a superb manner. Confident, but not too confident. Very helpful, very persuasive, very entertaining – and yet I always had the impression he was holding something back. He never overplayed his hand. If he hadn't been a salesman I think he could have made a good politician – or a spy . . .'

In my wine-fugged state, I found it pretty difficult to relate to this portrait of Dad. It was as though Gerald were talking about a stranger: David Harrison, Export Sales Director, rather than my dad. It wasn't that Dad never displayed those qualities when he was with us, but that important aspects of Dad's character were conspicuous by their absence from Gerald's glowing tribute. Irritation for a start. Obstinacy too. And, of course, the other, darker side of the entertaining sense of humour that Gerald so admired: the sarcasm. All of these were essential in any portrait of Dad. The rough and the smooth . . . I liked the idea of

Dad being a spy, though. It gave him a kind of distinction.

While I was mulling over Gerald's words, Mario arrived with our main courses. The baked mackerel smelt wonderful. Gerald poured us each another glass of wine. I'm not much of a drinker . . . two glasses of wine or cider's about my limit. Yet here I was knocking it back like there was no tomorrow. I was feeling pretty pissed, but pretty high too. Now there were two 'me's. An inside one and an outside one. The outside one was a bit addled, struggling with his words, actions and thoughts. The inside one was much more alert. He tried to keep the outside one in check – 'You're drunk,' he said now, and, 'For God's sake get your eyes in focus.' His voice was getting weaker, though, by the minute . . .

While we ate, Gerald and I traded affectionate anecdotes about Dad. Gerald did most of the talking. He told me about the early days, some office stories and Dad's views on various foreign peoples – which I'd heard plenty of times from Dad himself. To Dad, the Germans were very efficient, but rather inflexible; the Italians (dead masters like Longhi excluded, of course) were extremely inefficient, inconsistent and just plain infuriating; but the French, ah, the French, they were just about perfection – not as cold as the English, more flexible than the Germans, more reliable than the Italians and with a logic and passion all their own. Dad had a lot of time for the French.

Gerald told me that Dad had been responsible just about single-handedly for building up a substantial and very lucrative market in France for UKA's products. Apparently, the company was very worried about what would happen now that Dad was no longer around. I told Gerald about all the souvenirs Dad used to bring back from his trips, and the curious items he collected. I must have been pretty drunk, because I even went on at some length about the bird jug.

By the time coffee was mentioned, I was well in need of it. Liqueurs were mentioned, but with a last gust of willpower I managed to say no: a cappuccino would be fine. After the second coffee had gone down, though, my head was still feeling pretty fuzzy and I was also starting to feel very sleepy. I yawned, and Gerald asked me something about sleeping problems. And then, out of the blue, the inner me (as a last gesture before it nodded off) came up with the question that had been nagging at me since my interview with Donnelly earlier.

'On the day of the . . . when Mum and Dad were killed, was Dad going off on a trip?' I asked.

Suddenly, Gerald's whole expression and manner changed. He became very serious; he looked uneasy. He toyed with his coffee cup for a moment, turning it through a hundred and eighty degrees, as though he had something to say but wasn't quite sure how to say it. Then he looked me straight in the eye and said, 'There's something, Robert, that you ought to know about your father . . .'

Gerald told me that during the last couple of years Dad had been involved with a very important project at the company. A project that, Gerald claimed, could mean an awful lot – not only in UKA, but to the whole country. He couldn't tell me exactly what that project was – it was highly confidential – but apparently it had something to do with the development of a new and very revolutionary form of foil. Something that would widen foil applications enormously.

Gerald's stiffness relaxed a little and his face took on the wide-eyed look of the enthusiast. The sort of look you see on the faces of train-spotters when they start talking about steam engines.

'Aluminium, as you probably know, Robert,' he continued, 'is a very versatile material. Most people think of it as something used in catering and pharmaceuticals. But what they don't realize is the vital role it plays in so many areas of modern industrial life – telecommunications cables, building insulation, car radiators, aircraft construction even. It's *the* material of modern living. And this new form of foil that we've developed will open up untapped and extremely lucrative markets for UKA – and provide an awful lot of jobs.'

I looked at Gerald uncomprehendingly, wondering where his sales pitch was leading. What he was saying didn't seem to bear any relation to my question – in fact it didn't really seem to bear any relation to what we'd been talking about so far at all. Gerald fiddled with his coffee cup again. Then he said, 'The thing is, Robert, that your father played a vital part in developing this new foil and I'm certain he'd want to see everything possible done now to make sure it was a success . . . Well, we think he had some vital project data with him at home the day he and your mother were murdered . . . We're still a year or so away from manufacturing the actual product, so any leak now, as I'm sure you can appreciate, could well be disastrous . . .'

I still couldn't get my mind to operate as clearly as I'd have liked, but the two 'me's were starting to come back together. I suddenly felt very hot. A sense of alarm.

'What are you saying?' I asked. 'I don't understand what you're saying to me. This new foil stuff . . . Are you trying to tell me that it had something to do with Mum and Dad being killed?'

Gerald lifted his hands.

'No,' he said firmly, 'no, I'm not saying that.'

His heavy eyebrows had once more formed themselves into a *V* and the look in his eyes was sterner now –

sort of accusing, the kind of look teachers give you when they're about to tear you off a strip.

'Listen, Robert,' he said. 'Listen. What I am saying to you is that *if* the competitors were to get hold of the documents your father had in his possession, it would be very awkward for a lot of people in the company and very detrimental to the country as a whole. The government itself is involved and that is why it is vital that we find those papers . . . It is possible that they have already been taken . . .'

I was about to butt in again, but Gerald held his hand up again.

'We're pretty sure that that isn't the case.'

'But you're not sure,' I said. 'Which means . . .'

Trying simultaneously to puzzle out and express just what I thought it did mean demanded monumental effort. No maths problem at school had ever been this taxing. Or this important.

'Which means that, if those documents are missing, then Mum and Dad were murdered because of them . . .'

It was only after I'd finished speaking that the meaning of what I'd just said hit me. It filled me with horror. I leant forward, half-raised, my palms pressed down hard on the table, suddenly wide awake and stone-cold sober.

'Jesus!' I said. 'What is all this?'

Gerald moved his head from side to side, looking anxiously around the restaurant.

'Look, Robert, nothing is that certain,' he said, in a tone that was obviously meant to try and calm me down. 'Until we know for sure whether the documents are or are not missing we cannot say. There is certainly no indication whatsoever that the documents were involved in your parents' deaths. Quite the reverse, in fact. From what I have read it seems that your parents' valuable antiques were the cause.'

His eyebrows relaxed and the warmth came back again into his eyes.

'I really didn't mean to upset you more than you obviously are already,' he said. 'I'm sorry. I just wanted to ask you a favour . . .'

I sat back in my seat again.

'You want me to look for the documents,' I said.

Gerald nodded. 'Yes,' he said.

'But won't the police already have searched the house for them?' I asked.

'We'd prefer that the police weren't involved,' Gerald said. 'As I said, Robert, this matter is highly confidential.'

I felt lousy. My insides were all churned up. I didn't know what to think, what to say. Eventually I said, 'OK.'

'Thank you,' said Gerald.

Then he added something about Dad being proud of me. And a couple of other things. But I wasn't taking anything in now. I just wanted to get out of that place. I just wanted to go home. I felt overwhelmed. Like I'd woken from one awful nightmare only to find myself pitched into another.

I needed some time to think.

The nightmare only got worse on the car journey home. But even that was nothing to what followed when I finally got there. I felt terrible. My head was spinning, I was sweating, my stomach was heaving like I was on a hover-craft crossing a choppy sea . . . I was tired, but too disturbed to sleep. As soon as I closed my eyes to ease the spinning, a storm of disjointed words and thoughts flew chaotically through my head – as though my brain had gone on to automatic pilot. I couldn't recall ever in my life feeling as bad as I felt then. I ended up, half an hour or so later, with my head bowed over the toilet bowl, emptying out my undigested and very expensive lunch. Puking up's not exactly fun at the best of times – even if it does bring some sort of relief – but on this occasion it was particularly miserable. I suppose I'd always been used to having someone there to comfort me: Mum. Now I was all alone. 'Oh, God,' I whimpered. 'Oh, God.' I don't think there can be anything more desperate or lonely or just plain unpleasant than kneeling in the dark over a toilet bowl, puking your guts out with no one around to hear or care . . .

I passed a dreadful night and a pretty lousy day after it. I didn't get up – except to go to the toilet – until five o'clock in the afternoon. It was pitch-black outside by then. I made myself a cup of very strong coffee and sat at the kitchen table to drink it. The house was absolutely freezing, so I turned the central heating on. It took me a while to work out how to do it – which made me realize again just how much I'd relied on my parents . . . I'd never even turned the central heating on before; it was bloody ridiculous. How the hell was I going to be able to cope on my own?

It was more than a day now since my lunch with Gerald Finch, but not a moment had gone by, either waking or sleeping, without fragments of our conversation surfacing in my mind. It wasn't just the words either; it was the way Gerald had looked. There was something about the way he'd talked and the way his expression had changed so totally towards the end of our conversation that made me feel there was much more to this business about Dad and the new project than he'd let on. I felt like he was holding something back. What he *had* told me had been shocking enough. It seemed to open the whole case up, to introduce a completely new set of disturbing possibilities which I didn't really want to have to cope with. But I had to.

What if Mum and Dad had been killed because of the

documents Dad had? What if it hadn't been professional art thieves like Donnelly thought? And yet, surely, I thought, no one would commit murder for a few documents about foil – however revolutionary. I just couldn't make head or tail of any of it. The only thing I could do, I decided, was try to find those documents. I wasn't certain that I believed they existed. I suspected that even if they did, then they wouldn't be around the house still – if, indeed, they ever had been; but I wouldn't know for sure unless I did what Gerald had asked and looked. I had to do something anyway. Otherwise I'd just go crazy.

I spent the whole of that evening and the next day searching the house. I looked everywhere – upstairs and down – but I didn't find any UKA documents, highly confidential or otherwise. I did find all sorts of family documents, though, and things that I'd never seen before – my parents' wedding certificate, some old family photographs, a tatty ration book which had belonged to my grandparents . . . But most moving and interesting of all was a bundle of letters Dad wrote Mum from Australia about fifteen years ago, when he'd gone there on a long business trip. 'My darling Pam' or even 'My dearest darling Pam' was the affectionate way they all began; it made me realize how rarely I'd heard Dad use terms of endearment of any kind – especially in recent years. The letters were so affectionate, so touching, I could hardly bear to read them.

Some time in the evening Uncle Jim phoned for about the fifth time to see how I was. I told him I'd been feeling pretty bad but was OK now. I didn't tell him about meeting Gerald or what he'd said. I just didn't feel like going into it. He asked me how much longer I was going to stay at home and I said a couple of days more. Then he asked if I wanted some company, but I said I was feeling rather tired and was about to go to bed. It was an excuse, because I wanted to be on my own, but it was also true – I was feeling really knackered and I actually did go to bed when I got off the phone. But, as it turned out, I didn't get much sleep and I did have company . . .

I was awoken by a noise. It seemed to come from downstairs (I'd finally decided to forsake the sofa for the comfort of my own bed). I looked at the clock. It was nearly two o'clock. I listened hard and thought for a moment that either I must have been dreaming or that the wind had blown something over in the garden – or maybe that's just what I wanted to believe. But then I heard another noise – a sort of squeak and scrape. And it definitely came from inside the house, downstairs. It was the sound of my mum's bureau drawer in the sitting room being opened. The drawer was stiff and gave out a very distinctive sound when opened. There was no mistaking it.

I froze. I just lay there, propped up on my arm, listening, too scared to move – almost too frightened to breathe in case I made a noise and alerted the attention of the intruders. Then I started to think. I thought about the previous break-in and how that had ended; I thought about those papers and the look on Gerald's face; I thought my time was up . . . I heard voices in the hallway and looked around the room for somewhere to hide. But if whoever was downstairs made a thorough search, as it seemed they intended, then there was nowhere for me to hide.

I got out of bed quietly, and very stiffly pulled on my jeans. I could feel the goose pimples forming on my arms as my bare flesh met the chilly night air. I put on my T-shirt and sweater and slipped on a pair of shoes. I was still petrified, but I was at phase two of my scared-rabbit act – if after freezing you're still alive, then run like hell. I had to keep on my toes. My life might well depend upon it. I went to my bedroom doorway and stood there, listening. It was very quiet again now. Maybe they'd heard me getting out of bed. Standing there in the cold, I could feel every thumping beat of my heart and the sweat moistening my palms.

Then, suddenly, there was a loud crash as something

hit the floor downstairs. Instinctively I started to run. But I'd only taken a couple of paces when my left leg hit the ottoman that was on the landing and I tripped and fell with a thud to the floor. For a moment I just lay there, paralysed with fear again, unable to move, expecting the worst and cursing my clumsiness. I heard an exclamation of surprise from downstairs and I waited for the sound of ascending footsteps moving in for the kill. But they didn't come. The movements I heard seemed to be going away from me – out of the house.

I got to my feet quickly and ran downstairs. Suddenly I felt much tougher, defiant, reckless, angry. In an instant I'd found myself transformed from hunted to hunter and I took up the chase, without thinking. I sprinted out, through the open front door, along the pathway and into the street. Ahead of me I could see two shadowy figures running. I charged after them. I don't know why it is, but when you run at night you always seem to be moving much quicker than in daylight. And now I felt like I was flying. I wasn't thinking about what would happen if and when I caught up with my quarry (if I had done, I probably would have stopped dead), I just kept driving myself on towards them – and I seemed to be gaining. I *was* gaining. On one of them, anyway.

Their car was parked just beyond the mouth of our cul-de-sac. One of them reached it well before the other.

In a little more than a couple of seconds, he'd opened the car door, jumped in and started the engine. His partner, who looked too overweight to be very fit, was flagging though. By the time he reached the car I was almost on him. I could hear the heavy panting of his breath. I drove myself on harder. *I've got you*, I thought. He reached the car just ahead of me. The car door swung open. But instead of getting in, he turned round. His action took me by surprise so that I ran into him and I was already off balance when his fist hit me, hard, on the side of the head. I fell to the ground and he turned to get into the car. I grabbed his leg in a vain attempt to drag him back. He called out angrily – something that sounded like 'Ahmed' – then he shook his foot clear of my grasp and kicked me hard in the ribs and again in the stomach. I doubled up, more winded than in pain.

By the time I was able to look up once more, the car was at the end of the road. I saw its brake lights flash red momentarily, heard the squeal of its tyres as it rounded the corner, and that was that. It was gone. I lay there, coughing, half on the pavement, half in the road. Then I threw up noisily in the gutter. I felt lousy.

A neighbour found me lying in the road and called the police and an ambulance. My ribs ached a bit and my face really throbbed, but, as it turned out, I looked in a worse state than I really was. Nothing terrible showed up on the X-rays they gave me at the hospital and, after a thorough examination, I was reassured by a jolly young doctor that there was nothing broken, no cracked ribs even – I'd just have to put up with looking like a giraffe for a week or so. He didn't mean by this that my neck had suddenly grown – he was referring, in his jokey way, to the browny-yellow blotches that, he assured me, would soon become very prominent on my body and around my right eye. I didn't laugh.

Uncle Jim came to the hospital – the police called him. He was pretty shaken-up, not his usual blustery self at all. He laid into the police pretty hard, doing his 'I'm a local councillor and I demand immediate action' bit – wanted to know when they were going to catch these thugs, and when they were going to get Mum and Dad's murderers, and make the area a safe place to live in again. I actually found myself feeling sorry for the police officer who was taking my statement. He didn't look a lot older than I was and he was about a million times more considerate than Detective Sergeant Barnes had been. We'd been getting on fine, before Uncle Jim arrived.

Everyone tried to persuade me not to return home, but to stay at Uncle Jim's – for the night at least. But I wouldn't have it. The night's events had given me a new strength, an anger and a determination not to be beaten, not to be bullied away from my own home. God knows, I didn't have much left to cling to.

'Come on, Robert. These people aren't playing, you know,' Uncle Jim coaxed. 'Don't be so pig-headed.'

But from now on, I thought, that's exactly what I am going to be – bloody obstinate . . . just like Dad.

I've just been given a pat on the back from Sigmund for being 'so co-operative and honest' . . . But he should know that nothing's as straightforward as that. I bloody well know, and that's for sure. People can be obstructive and lie, I told him, and yet still somehow believe they're being co-operative and honest. They aren't two sides of the same coin, they're two sides of the same image on the same face. Maybe I'm lying now. Maybe everything I've said's been a lie. Why should it be true, just because I say it and it's down in ink? I asked him how he could be certain I was remembering correctly. No one can recall whole conversations perfectly, word for word, can they? I said. Sigmund seems to think that doesn't really matter. He says he wants me to relive my experiences, not recall them. But that just sounds like hair-splitting to me. It's like when you read a novel and the author tells you this and that about a character, and you think – or at least *I* *think* – That's what *you* say, that's what *you* think, but why should I take your word for it? I tried to explain that to an English teacher at school once, but he just burbled on about the conventions of fiction and the omniscient narrator and stuff – while ignoring or simply refusing to understand my real point. Which was: if you don't think you can believe anything you read, how can you go on reading? It was a point I made again in more than one of my English GCSE papers. Perhaps that's why I only just managed to scrape through.

It was Mum's turn to be put under Sigmund's spotlight today. First of all, though, he asked me how I thought my parents got on. He said that he got the impression from what I'd said so far that there had been increasing family tensions. I said that there were tensions in every family. Dad could be pretty sarcastic and Mum was volatile – so naturally there were tensions. That didn't mean they didn't get on, though. Sigmund said he wondered if I wasn't being a little defensive. I told him I wondered if *he* wasn't being a little bit of a bloody Hitler. We left it at that.

Sigmund said he'd got a pretty clear picture of Dad from what I'd said so far, but that Mum was much more shadowy. So I talked about Mum, while Sigmund sat there, like he always does, leaning well back in his chair – very laid back, but at the same time very attentive, hardly saying a word and yet saying just enough to prompt me into telling him what he wants to know. Sometimes it feels like he's a priest and the room a kind of confessional.

I started by giving Sigmund a kind of physical description of Mum. She was quite tall and slim, with fair hair. I don't know whether you'd call her pretty or not. I thought she was – but then I was her son. Elegant is the word I'd use to describe her, I think. She could be moody like Dad, but her moods were much more open than his. If she was angry, you knew it straight away. She didn't bother much with sarcasm or irony or anything devious like that. And likewise when she was pleased or happy, she made it very plain. Either way, I think you could say she was a pretty decisive person.

Sigmund asked me to tell him something more about her. Any anecdotes, memories . . . The first thing that came to mind. So I told him about a couple of incidents that happened a long time ago, when I was just a kid.

One time, when I was about five or so, I was playing with a friend of mine called Johnny. We were having a great time playing with our collection of toy cars – we'd built a garage out of Lego and everything. Anyway, it got to nearly dinner time and Mum came in and said we had to pack up our toys and get ready to eat. Then out she went – and we carried on playing. About five minutes later she came back, pretty angry, and said that if we didn't finish playing and clear up right away, she'd put all of the toys in a black sack and give them away to the local charity shop. Then she went out. Well, of course we started to clear up after that, but then I suddenly had a brilliant idea for improving the garage and had to show Johnny and . . . when Mum came back again she found us totally absorbed with our garage improvements and toy cars still all over the floor. 'Right,' she said, 'I warned you.' She marched out and came back a moment later with a big black sack into which, before our horrified and disbelieving eyes, she bundled all of our cars and our prized garage. Then she took them away – and that was the last I ever saw of them.

The other thing I told Sigmund happened when I was about nine or ten. I was in my penultimate year at primary school. The school football team was composed of boys in the year above, but there was one place unfilled. The football coach gave us boys in the year below a sort of penalty-taking test – and I won. So I was in the team. Only they'd forgotten about this one boy who'd been ill when they'd been picking the team. And when he came back to school, a couple of days later, the coach decided he should be in the team instead of me. When I got home that afternoon I cried my eyes out. It seemed so unfair. Mum listened and comforted me. Then she got in the car and drove to the school and talked to the headmaster. I don't know what she said to him, but I got my place back in the team. I thought she was the most wonderful mother in the world. It seemed like there was nothing she couldn't fix. I was as proud of her then as I'd been appalled when she'd given away my toy cars. But then I was still young enough to believe in the virtual infallibility of grown-ups . . .

And none of *this* had happened.

The next day I had another interview with Donnelly and told him all about my conversation with Gerald. I told him too my suspicions that Gerald was holding something back – that there was more to this than he'd let on. Donnelly wrinkled his moustache quite a bit and nodded his big head and wandered around the sitting room, as he had the last time he'd been in the house. He seemed pretty interested in what I told him. Forensics, he told me, had done various tests around the place, but hadn't yet come up with anything very useful – no 'foreign' finger-prints or anything. I wasn't able to be much use with descriptions of the intruders either, because I'd only really seen them from behind, in the dark. That one was quite a lot bigger than the other was about all I could say for certain. But I was able to report what the big one had said and my idea that it might have been the other one's name.

'Ahmed, you say,' Donnelly pondered. 'Well, there

might be something in that. It's not a very usual name – not in this country, anyway. I think I told you my feelings about the unusual.'

I nodded. Then I asked him, 'Do you think this has something to do with my parents' murder?'

'It is possible,' he said. 'I hope we'll have a clearer idea about that once I've spoken to your Mr Finch. I'm not a great believer in coincidence myself. Two break-ins in as many months at the same house . . . It seems likely they'd be connected, doesn't it? And yet, well . . . We'll have to wait and see – and hope, of course. One must never lose hope.'

That word again. Donnelly, it seemed to me, did an awful lot of hoping.

Then he suddenly started on another tack.

'It's a shame about the bird,' he said, glancing at the Martinware jug, where it stood on the bookshelf, with one wing broken off. That had been the cause of the crash I'd heard the night before. I looked at the bird, then I looked at Donnelly. There was something too slow and calm and unconcerned about him. His tone was no different now when talking about a broken ornament – albeit a valuable one – than it had been when discussing Mum and Dad's murder. His air of detachment irked me and I lost my temper.

'Look,' I said vehemently, 'I don't give a stuff about the

bird. Bugger the bird . . . I just want you to find my parents' killer. That's all.'

I might as well have saved my breath. There was no way Donnelly was going to change his manner or his methods of investigation. I knew that really. I just ended up looking stupid for my outburst. But at least I hadn't allowed myself to be pushed into exchanging trite chitchat, the kind of meaningless cringe-making drivel that adults always try to engage you in at 'grown-up' parties . . . Well, this was no social occasion and I wasn't going to let Donnelly or anyone else treat it like one.

When Donnelly went, he left a uniformed policeman on guard in the street. I sat down on the sofa and tried to pull my thoughts together. The police and forensics team had left the place looking even more of a mess than it had after the break-in of the night before. I was getting tired of all these destructive intrusions. Each one had taken away a little more of the sanctity and security that made the house home; how could you feel homely in a place where anyone who felt like it could stroll in and steal or smash or murder or generally rearrange the place at will? About the only thing that seemed to have remained constant and untouched by the various intrusions of the past couple of months was that sublime Longhi print on the wall. If those four silent scholarly witnesses could speak, I thought, what a terrible tale they would tell . . .

I picked up the broken bird jug and turned it round in my hands. It was no longer a joke, it was pathetic with its one wing. If Mum had been around, she would have been overjoyed at finally having an excuse to get rid of it; but Dad would have been mad – and heaven help whoever had broken it. I was mad too now. And top of the list of things I was mad at just now was Gerald, the 'bird man' himself.

The more I thought about it, the more I was becoming convinced that the two break-ins had to be linked and that Mum and Dad had been murdered because of that secret project. I was pretty sure now too that Gerald had been behind the break-in the night before. I reckoned that maybe he hadn't trusted me to search the place properly, so he'd sent some of his men to do the job. Him and his bloody secret projects. He could keep them. But also he could keep his hands off my home.

It was strange, though, that the same men who'd robbed and murdered my parents in cold blood just two months before could be scared into running off like rabbits by the sound of a mere thud – as had happened the night before. Perhaps they'd thought it was a trap. But would such cold-blooded professional killers have allowed me to get as close to them as I had – well within identification range – and let me live? OK, so one of them had given me a bit of a beating (my face still throbbed and I had a shiner developing), but he hadn't tried to shoot me or anything.

Whatever the solution, it seemed to me that Gerald Finch held the key to my discovering it. He was holding something back, I was sure of it, and if Donnelly didn't get it out of him, then, somehow, I would have to try. I had no idea how.

If only, I thought, I could find those documents . . .

I don't know why I thought of it. I was just sitting there, reliving some childhood memories, recalling some good times with Mum and Dad . . . when a picture came into my head of Dad making me my very own secret hidey-hole. I was about seven, and into secret agents and stuff. Dad chiselled this little compartment in the wall at the back of the cupboard in my room where I kept my toys and things. It had a proper door, covered with wallpaper so that − to the casual glance anyway − it was pretty invisible. It only went back about a couple of inches or so, but it was nearly a foot in height. I used to keep my secret-agent gear in there − badge, wallet, fountain-pen transmitter, gun . . . I kept my diary in there for a while too, and letters. Once, when I was about thirteen, it housed a pornographic magazine. I hadn't used it − or thought about it even − for years. But I was thinking about it now. And wondering. It was just about the only place left in the whole house that I hadn't checked out.

I went upstairs to my bedroom and opened the cupboard door. It was full of books, old games, paper, bits of this and that . . . I pulled a load out until I had easy access to the concealed door at the back. It didn't have a handle, so it was difficult to open. In the end, I put a penknife blade in the crack at the side and prised it open. I'm not sure what I expected to find, but I have to admit I was a bit disappointed when all I pulled out was a book.

I thought for a moment that maybe it was just something I'd left in there. But it wasn't any book of mine. It was an old, leather-bound volume, written in French, entitled *Thérèse Raquin*, by Émile Zola. I'd heard of the book, because it had been dramatized on TV some years ago, but I had no idea what it was about. Not that I supposed it would have been of much consequence if I had. The point was, I'd hoped for documents and found some old book. I opened it up, then held it upside down, but nothing fell out. Then I shook it a bit, hopefully . . . And something did drop out.

It was a photograph. A photograph of a woman standing in an alley of rather spindly, bare trees in what looked like a park of hard sand. There was some kind of statue in the background and a hedge. I looked more closely at the woman. I didn't recognize her. I turned the photo over to see if there was anything written on the back. There wasn't. I turned back to look at the woman again. She looked about thirty-five – or older maybe; I'm lousy at ages. She was very well and expensively dressed. She wore a mink coat and some very ostentatious gold jewellery. Her hair was very blonde – so blonde that, although I couldn't see any roots, I thought it must have been bleached. She was very attractive, in a hard sort of way, with a slightly mocking smile. But who was she? And what was her photograph doing in this old book? And why was this old book hidden in a secret compartment at the back of my cupboard? It had something to do with Dad, I was sure of that much at least. He was the secret one in our family – and the one who collected books. And the only one who could read novels in French.

I spent the rest of the morning going through the book, page by page, looking for any sort of clue that would help me to find an answer to my questions – some words scribbled in a margin, a passage underlined – but the only thing resembling a message was an inscription printed on the ornate sticker which adorned the inside front cover. There was a motto in Latin, which I didn't understand, followed by the name of a school, *L'École de Sainte Catherine*, a girl's name, Mlle Marie Calimet, and the date, *Novembre 1883*. All of which told me nothing.

I was convinced that the book was important – crucial even. It had to be. Why else would Dad have hidden it in such an obscure and secret place? And then there was the fact that when I'd disturbed the intruders the night before, they'd almost certainly been searching the book-shelves. I knew that from the broken bird. But why was the book so important? I just couldn't puzzle it out. What I needed, I eventually decided, was some expert help. From someone who knew what they were talking about. Which meant Aunty Barbara.

Barbara Wallace – or 'Aunty' Barbara as I'd always known her – owned the antiques shop that Mum had worked in and was Mum's oldest and closest friend. I knew she'd be pleased to see me. And I was sure that she'd help me if she could. I still felt a bit embarrassed about what had happened at the funeral, but I'd just have to brush that aside.

Wallace Antiques was about fifteen minutes' walk away, in the centre of town. It was a smart but cosy place. In the window, classy items like solid-silver ornaments or rare prints sat side by side with less valuable bric-a-brac objects – and, quite frequently, Barbara's fluffy Burmese cat, Nathaniel. He was there today, sitting quite still, looking out on the world as though, quite honestly, it didn't really matter. I'd never envied him his detachment more than I did now, as I pushed open the door and heard the familiar tinkle of the bell. As I did so, I felt an almost crippling pang of anguish and loss: for this was

Mum's world and when I came here I came to see Mum –
but now Mum was gone.

Aunty Barbara was at the back of the shop, polishing
some silver candlesticks. She looked over when I came
in. My first impression was that she seemed older and
greyer than I remembered her.

'Robert!' she exclaimed. 'Oh, Robert!'

She took off her glasses and came over to me with her
arms outstretched. Then she gave me a big hug, pulling
my head down on to her shoulder. She held me like that
for what seemed ages. I could feel my neck muscles
tighten and my chest hurt like hell. But then, when she
finally let go and I saw the tears in her eyes, I felt guilty for
having thought of anything so mundane as bodily
discomfort.

'Oh, Robert,' she said. 'What have they done to you?'
And she touched my face gently, where the bruise was.

'It's nothing, Aunty Barbara,' I said. 'Just a black eye,
that's all. I'll explain later.'

'It's terrible,' she said, shaking her head. 'This whole
thing. What kind of awful world are we living in?'

She took my hand and squeezed it, sighing.

'Come on,' she said. 'Come and sit down. I'll put the
kettle on. Sometimes it seems as though tea's about
the only sure bastion we've got left.'

While we drank our tea, Aunty Barbara asked me how

I was and what I'd been doing since the funeral – how I'd been coping, what I felt, and about the black eye, of course. I did my best to answer her questions, but as I spoke, I was struck by how unreal, how unbelievable it all sounded – as though it had happened to someone else, or as though I were describing a dream. I told her what I could recall of my sedated days at Uncle Jim's and about my lunch with Gerald Finch and the previous night's break-in and the scuffle that followed – which brought us to the subject of the book and the main reason I'd come.

'Well, let's take a look,' she said. 'Books aren't my speciality, of course, but I might be able to tell you a thing or two.'

I passed her the book. She put on her glasses and peered at the cover, frowning with concentration, as though she were trying to place a hallmark or something.

'*Thérèse Raquin*,' she read. 'That's Émile Zola, isn't it? Or is it Victor Hugo? I'm always getting the two of them mixed up.'

She turned to the title page.

'No,' she said. 'I was right the first time. Émile Zola. Well, Robert, what would you like to know?'

'Anything,' I said. 'Everything. Whatever you can tell me, Aunty Barbara.'

'I can tell you the story, if that would help.'

'Yes, please,' I said.

So Aunty Barbara told me the story of *Thérèse Raquin*. It's about a woman, Thérèse, and her lover, Laurent, and what happens to them and their relationship after they murder Thérèse's husband. What does happen to them, basically, is that they go to pieces – a bit like Macbeth and Lady Macbeth – and start having really morbid and guilty thoughts. They get married, thinking that being together will make them feel better, but in fact it just makes things worse – and soon they can't stand each other's guts. In the end, things get so bad that they commit suicide.

'It's not a very happy story,' Aunty Barbara concluded. 'But there you are. That's nineteenth-century French literature for you.'

It struck me that real contemporary life wasn't exactly a bundle of laughs either. But I kept my gloomy thoughts to myself.

I asked Aunty Barbara if there was anything more she could tell me about the book, as an object, rather than its contents. She turned to the title page once more.

'Well,' she said. 'It's not a first edition. Not even a second, in fact. See, there's the date of the original printing – 1867. And the second. And then this one. Still, it might be worth a little, I suppose. Only . . .' She peered at the book more closely. Then she turned it over and looked hard at the book's spine.

'This isn't the original cover. It looks to me like the book's been rebound and this leather cover has been added. It's something book dealers do quite a lot. Some dealer probably picked this up in a terrible condition, repaired it and slapped on a new cover. Then made a big profit on it, no doubt. Still, we all do it, I suppose, to some extent.'

'But what about the sticky label inside?' I said. 'The date on that's 1883. So how can the cover have been added?'

'Oh, that,' she said. 'That, I imagine, is a fake. Or a genuine *ex libris* label transferred from another book. Another piece of deception, I'm afraid, Robert.'

I showed Aunty Barbara the photograph I'd found in the book. But she didn't recognize the woman. I hadn't really thought she would. I wasn't at all sure that the photograph wasn't a red herring anyway. I'd bought plenty of books at jumble sales in my time and found slips of paper or photographs somewhere between the pages. Maybe this was the same kind of thing. Aunty Barbara peered again at the photograph.

'No,' she said. 'I definitely don't know her. The background seems familiar though. It looks like the Tuileries.'

'The Tuileries?' I queried.

'The Tuileries Gardens in Paris,' she explained. 'Near the Louvre. I'd say that's where this photograph was taken. Well, that would tally with the French book, wouldn't it?'

I agreed that it would. But I wasn't sure that it helped me any.

There was something else I had to talk to Aunty Barbara about before I left. Something which I knew would probably be a bit painful for us both. But there were things I needed to know about that awful afternoon; things which only Aunty Barbara could tell me – because she'd been just about the last person to see Mum alive. I wanted to know how she'd been, what she'd said – any scrap that might bring her to life again, even if only for a moment, and help make things a little more bearable.

Aunty Barbara told me what she remembered, as best she could, her voice gradually getting more and more unsteady and emotional.

'It was all so normal,' she said. 'Everything was so utterly normal. Pam was very jolly. We talked about all sorts of things. I recall we laughed for ages about a hideous gilt chamber pot that I'd picked up at an auction the day before. Pam said it looked like a throne.'

'Did she talk about me at all, Aunty Barbara?' I asked.

'Yes,' she said. 'She said something about your exams. About your doing well in . . . geography, was it?'

I nodded.

'She said she was afraid you were going to get awfully

swollen-headed about it and rest on your laurels. I said that if you'd done well then you deserved to. She said that was the *only* thing you'd done well in . . . I got the feeling from what she said that your father wasn't too pleased with your results.'

'No,' I said. 'Not exactly.'

'And then he called,' Aunty Barbara continued.

I looked at her in surprise.

'Dad called?'

'Yes. I don't know what he called about, but it seemed to take Pam by surprise. She went very quiet. Then, when she came off the phone, she said she had to go. "I've got to dash, Babs," she said. Then she picked up her coat and off she went. And that was the last I saw of her.'

'You don't have any idea what Dad called about, do you?' I asked.

Aunty Barbara shook her head.

'No, Robert, I don't. The police asked me the same thing. I did get the impression that he wanted Pam to go home for some reason though. Urgently.'

'Mum didn't say anything about what Dad was doing at home? I mean, he should have been at work.'

'All she said was that she had to go,' said Aunty Barbara sadly. 'I've thought about that telephone call a lot over the last couple of months. You see, if your father hadn't called, then Pam might still have been alive today.

And if he hadn't been at home, then they would both be alive. It's as though some cruel fate had marked their cards. It all seems so horribly . . . unfair.'

Aunty Barbara looked at me with watery eyes.

'Oh, Robert, Robert, I'm so sorry,' she said, and hugged me to her again, like she had when I'd first come in. I stood there holding her, listening to her crying, not knowing how to console her, but holding her tightly, the way Mum had many times held me, the way she'd held me that day when I'd come home upset about the football team, as though she were sheltering me against life's injustices. I stood there holding Aunty Barbara, a woman thirty years my senior, trying to soothe her grief.

'It's OK, Aunty Barbara,' I said. 'It's OK.' I knew when I was saying it how stupid it sounded. But it was just sounds, soothing sounds. Sounds I'd heard Mum make when she'd been comforting me.

I suddenly felt about a hundred years old.

When I got back to the house, the first thing I did was to phone Donnelly. It took them a while to locate him, but they found him eventually. I asked him if he'd spoken to Gerald. He had. I waited in some anticipation for him to tell me that, as a result, the case had been cracked wide open. But he didn't say anything of the sort. Quite the reverse, in fact. In Donnelly's opinion Gerald Finch had had nothing to do with Dad's death and he suggested that I'd got the wrong end of the stick. He hinted that the combination of alcohol and emotional exhaustion often had the effect of distorting a person's interpretation of words and facts – which I quickly realized was a reference to myself, and the state I'd been in at my lunch with Gerald. Which meant that Gerald had told Donnelly but also that he'd lied about what he'd said about Dad and the secret project. I told Donnelly my thoughts, but he didn't sound very impressed. Gerald must have done a great job on him. There didn't seem any point in telling Donnelly about the book I'd found, bearing in mind his negative attitude.

Donnelly had something to ask me, though – and it took me quite by surprise.

'I wonder if I might ask you, Robert,' he began, in his usual stiff manner, 'if your father had an interest in shooting.'

'Shooting?' I repeated, incredulously.

'Yes, shooting,' said Donnelly. 'I take it from your tone that he didn't.'

'No,' I said. 'But why do you ask?'

'Well,' he said, 'it appears that your father recently purchased a revolver.'

'A revolver?' I said.

'Yes,' said Donnelly, 'and from what we know of the

gun, we believe it may have been the murder weapon.'

I tried desperately to take in all that Donnelly was saying. The information. The repercussions. But I couldn't.

'I don't understand,' I said. 'Dad never had a gun. If he did, why didn't I ever see it around the house? And where is it now?'

'Your father purchased the gun very recently,' said Donnelly. 'Just a week, in fact, before he was killed. As to where it is now . . . Well, it's wherever the murderers threw it – at the bottom of a river somewhere, I expect. I only wish I knew . . .'

Donnelly asked me a couple more questions about the gun and whether I had any idea why Dad had bought it – had he ever made mention of any threats against his life or Mum's or mine even? I hadn't any ideas. I couldn't help him. I was too dazed to think. And too pissed off about Gerald to consider it anyway. I had the impression that Donnelly, like Gerald, was keeping things from me. He wasn't really letting me in on his investigations. Well then, I wouldn't let him in on mine.

The gun was a real shock, there was no doubt about that. But on further reflection, I realized it gave further credence to what Gerald had told me. The little he'd told me. If Dad had bought a revolver, it certainly hadn't been for sport. I was pretty sure that the only shooting he'd ever done was with Uncle Jim's air pistol out in Uncle

Jim's back garden. And if he hadn't bought the gun for sport, then he must have got it for protective reasons. Which meant that he felt threatened by someone or something – and it was up to me to find out what. As far as I could see, the only lead I had was Gerald. And France . . . A French book, a French place, a French woman (?) and Dad's close links, obsession almost, with France. All roads, it seemed, led to Paris.

I phoned Gerald Finch at his office. He was very warm, very sincere, like before.

'I've got something for you,' I said.

'What do you mean, Robert?' he said smoothly. 'Are you telling me that you've found the documents?'

'Yes,' I lied. 'I've found them. I'll bring them to your office tomorrow.'

'Tomorrow's Saturday,' he said.

'All the better,' I said. 'It'll be more private.'

'Fine,' he said. 'Fine.' He paused for a moment. Then he said, 'You know, Robert, your father would be very proud of you.'

It was the second time in a couple of days that he'd made that claim. It was as though he saw my father's hypothetical pride in me as a carrot with which he could get me to do whatever he wanted.

'What time should I expect you?' he asked.

'Midday,' I said.

'I'll send a car for you,' he said.

But I said no. I didn't want to put myself in his hands.

'I'll come under my own steam,' I said.

'As you wish, Robert,' he said. And that was that.

It was only when I put down the receiver that I started to wonder if I was doing the right thing. Going to Gerald's office on my own . . . How could I be sure no one else would be there? Or know what might happen to me? But, all things considered, it seemed like a chance I had to take. If I met Gerald in public I'd be safer, but I'd probably have less opportunity of getting anything out of him than if we were on our own – and I was tired of not being told things. This time I was going to make an adult tell me the truth.

The games were over now: this time I was going to be armed . . .

We talked a bit about guns today – how I felt about them and stuff – and I told Sigmund about the time, when I was about eight or nine, that Uncle Jim showed me how to shoot an air pistol. Dad was there too. We went round to Uncle Jim's one Sunday morning. Usually we went swimming on Sunday mornings, but today, as a special treat, Dad and Uncle Jim were going to teach me how to shoot. It was a very cold day – late autumn or winter, I think – and I wore a thick sweater that my grandmother had knitted for me. (I remember that sweater really well; it had small checks of dark yellow, scored with red lines, and a black collar. It was the warmest sweater I've ever had. I wish I had it now. I wish I had it in my hands right now. I wonder what happened to it. I've got this sad suspicion that it's probably lying threadbare or unravelled in a corner somewhere. Like my life.)

There was still frost on the ground when we went out into Uncle Jim's garden. Uncle Jim and Dad had cups of steaming hot coffee. I had a mug of hot milk. The first thing Uncle Jim explained to me was that it was difficult to shoot with cold hands. It made your finger too stiff on the trigger, he said, and that's why the Lone Ranger wore gloves. He was just making a joke, I suppose, but I remember his remark puzzled me, because it seemed to me that it was just as hard to do things with gloves on as it was when the cold got in your joints.

The target was a tin can, perched on the back wall, just along from Uncle Jim's shed, where the gun itself was kept. I watched enthralled as Uncle Jim took the gun out of its box and unfurled the cloth that lay around it. The gun was black and squarish, almost Luger-like – very different from the cowboy pistol I had expected. It seemed very large too – too large for me to manage.

Dad and Uncle Jim took a few shots first, while I stood and watched. They laughed when Dad sent the can clattering off the wall. I laughed too. But a bit nervously – because I didn't want to shoot the gun any more. It was too big and I was scared that I wouldn't be able to fire it and would make a fool of myself. But soon it was my turn. Uncle Jim helped me to aim the gun and warned me about the recoil. Even so, though, when I pulled the trigger, the gun careered wildly and I lost control. God knows what happened to the pellet; it probably frightened some passing pigeon half to death.

Uncle Jim just laughed but Dad was annoyed, as I was afraid he would be.

'Hold tight, stupid,' he said, irritably. I wanted to cry. I felt so miserable, so humiliated. I wanted to throw the gun down and never touch it again. I hated it when he called me 'stupid'. I know there may seem to be lots of worse things that he could have called me, but 'stupid' was the worst of the lot for me. Mum called me 'silly' sometimes – but that was OK. That sounded sort of endearing. It was the way Dad said 'stupid'. With irritation and disappointment – the voice of a man who couldn't stand incompetence of any kind, not even in the form of his nine-year-old son making a bit of a balls-up of his first attempt at shooting. But then there was the other side – his genuine affection and pride when I subsequently succeeded in firing the gun somewhere in the direction of the target, even eventually hitting it. Then he made me feel like I was the world's greatest marksman. I felt happy and proud to be his son, because he seemed so happy and proud to be my father. It wasn't that way too often. Not in the last few years anyway.

The point is, though, I said to Sigmund, that's when I first learnt how to shoot. That's how I know how to handle a gun. And I think maybe it would have saved us all an awful lot of trouble if I'd just turned the gun to my head that first day and pulled the trigger. *BOY BLOWS BRAINS*

OUT WITH AIR PISTOL! The tabloids would have had a field day . . .

But, no, why should they get their grubby hands on me? Isn't it enough that they mauled my parents' memory, like jackals tearing at the flesh of a dead animal? Like the way Sigmund picks me clean, until I feel like a pile of fish bones on a plate: dissected, naked, no longer even an entire skeleton, but just a pathetic heap of bones . . .

I woke up early Saturday morning after a restless night, with a feeling of utter futility. I just lay there in bed for ages staring at the ceiling thinking negative thoughts about how stupid I was. Me, a sixteen-year-old boy, trying to do the job of the police force, setting out to discover his parents' killer . . . It was simply ridiculous.

I felt very alone. For just about the first time since this whole thing had happened I thought about school and the 'friends' I had there: Garth, Nick, Bozo, Lucy, Caroline . . . I wondered if I'd dropped out of their world as quickly and completely as they had dropped out of mine. None of them had made any great effort to get in contact – certainly not since I'd come back home anyway. It was as though I'd been removed from their lives as surely as I'd been removed from the school register . . . Did anyone even talk about me any more? I wondered. A picture came to me of the Old Fart making a reference in the staff room to 'that chap Harrison'. 'Shocking affair,' he'd say, slurping his tea. And the head would nod his head and look awkwardly at his shoes for a moment – and then they'd change the subject. 'The hockey team played rather well on Saturday,' the Old Fart would say (the school was rather hot at hockey). And the head would agree. And I'd be well and truly forgotten.

I got to the point where I was feeling so dispirited that I seriously considered giving up my whole plan and just going back to sleep. But then I thought about that broken bird and the empty places on the mantelpiece and in the cabinet where the thimbles and pottery figures and other things had been, and those elegant geography students looking down on me as though willing me to take from them the spirit of adventure that they themselves were unable to put into practice . . . and I knew I had to carry on, no matter how foolhardy or futile my actions might seem to be. So, eventually, I dragged myself out of bed.

The first thing I had to do was get hold of my weapon – Uncle Jim's air pistol. It was kept now in Uncle Jim's loft. I still had a key, so getting into the house would be no problem – but I needed to make sure that there wouldn't be anyone around. There probably wouldn't be, because Aunty Susan went out shopping most Saturday mornings, while Uncle Jim played golf. It was a hobby he'd taken up over the last few years as part of his political aspirations. In our suburb being 'in' at the golf club carried a lot of clout when it came to running for local office. 'Becoming mayor round here,' I'd heard him grumble, 'is not so much a matter of winning over your colleagues in the council chambers as impressing the old gin soaks in the clubhouse.' I phoned and there was no reply. The coast, it seemed, was clear.

Fifteen minutes later I was letting myself into Uncle Jim's house. Neither Uncle Jim's nor Aunty Susan's car was in the driveway so I was pretty certain that no one was home. I called out when I got inside – just in case. There was no reply. I put the copy of *Thérèse Raquin* on the windowsill by the front door and then had a quick look downstairs, just to make really certain there was no one around. Then I went upstairs. The entrance to the loft was in the ceiling, above the landing. I reached up with a pole and pulled its handle down. The loft door came open and a ladder slid down. I climbed up.

It took me a few minutes to find the light switch because it was down on the floor, between two beams. When I flicked it on, the naked bulb gave out a dingy, shadowy light, which barely touched the corners of the room. The loft was full of cardboard boxes covered in newspaper and dustsheets, and masses of dusty junk that obviously hadn't seen the light of day for years. But there was no sign of an air pistol. I took a deep breath and then started my search. The first thing I uncovered was a small silver Christmas tree that I remembered from my childhood. Uncle Jim and Aunty Susan used to put it up in their dining room, decorated with fairy lights. Dad and Mum and I used to come round on Christmas Eve for dinner, and it was always there, shining away in the background. It looked pretty sad now, lying there all dusty and dishevelled – lifeless without its lights.

I searched all the way along one wall and halfway round the next before I came upon what I was looking for – and by the time I did my hands were dry and filthy from dust and I was beginning to get a bit frantic. Then I threw back a huge dustsheet . . . and there it was, in a box, wrapped up in a cloth – like in the old days – so that all I could see was the butt. I bent down to pick it up. But as I did so, something else caught my eye. Something surprisingly clean and bright. Something extraordinarily familiar . . . A vase. A Ming vase.

I stared at it, mesmerized, for a moment. Then I pulled the dustsheet right off to look at it more closely. It certainly looked like Mum's vase – but then there was more than one Ming vase in the world, wasn't there? Of course there was . . . only . . . it did look an awful lot like Mum's. Still, I might just have passed it off as co-incidence, if I hadn't seen the thimble poking out of a bed of cotton wool where I'd disturbed the newspapers that had been covering it. And then I *knew* it was Mum's vase, and that the thimble was one of the Meissen thimbles Dad had given Mum – and that if I went on looking I'd find the ivory Madras chess set and the pottery figures too. All the stuff that had been taken in the robbery. Suddenly some really unpleasant thoughts came into my head. And then I heard the front door slam – and Uncle Jim's voice call out, 'Hello, darling, I'm back. Hello, are you there?'

I froze, listening for his footsteps on the stair. But they didn't come. I picked up the thimble and stuffed it in my pocket. Then I unwrapped the gun, shook out a handful of pellets from the box and loaded one into the chamber. It wasn't easy, because my hands were shaking with tension and fear. I crept over to the loft entrance and paused, listening for a moment. I could hear Uncle Jim downstairs in the kitchen – fixing himself a drink. I climbed down the ladder to the landing, then made my way slowly and quietly downstairs. The copy of *Thérèse Raquin* was still on the window ledge where I'd put it, so it looked as though Uncle Jim hadn't seen it. I heard the clink of ice in a glass. As I approached the kitchen, my feelings of fear became hardened by a rush of violent anger. I wanted to get the bastard.

He was by the sink with his back to me, when I came into the kitchen doorway.

'OK, you bastard,' I spat out. 'I'm going to give you a

taste of your own medicine.' I raised the gun and aimed it at his head. It was only an air pistol, but at short range an air pistol can do a lot of damage.

Uncle Jim jumped right out of his skin. The glass he'd been filling spun off the surface and smashed into pieces on the floor. There was a strong smell of gin. He turned round.

'What the . . . Christ, Robert!' he exclaimed. 'What the hell are you doing?' He was breathing heavily. 'You nearly gave me a heart attack.'

'I wouldn't want you to die that quickly,' I said.

The hand holding the gun was shaking now and I grasped it with my other one to try and keep my aim steady.

'What the hell are you on about? And what are you doing with my air pistol? What is this? Have you gone completely mad?' I noticed with some satisfaction the look of total shock in Uncle Jim's eyes. I'd really shaken him up.

'No,' I snarled, 'I haven't gone mad. I've just wised up. And *this* is all about revenge.'

'Revenge?' he said. 'Revenge? Revenge for what? For God's sake, Robert, what are you talking about?'

With the gun still raised in my right hand, and without taking my eyes off his for a moment, I reached down and took the thimble out of my pocket. I held it up in front of me.

'I'm talking about this,' I said. 'This is what I'm talking about . . . you bastard. How could you do it?' My voice was shaking now, almost as much as my hands. Even putting both of them on the butt, I couldn't hold the gun still.

He looked at the thimble for an instant, then he closed his eyes and took a deep breath.

'Oh, Christ,' he said. Then he looked at me. 'You've been in the loft, haven't you?' he asked softly.

'Yes,' I said, 'and I'm going to make you pay for what I found there, you murderer.'

The last words came out as a kind of shriek. I was losing control. My whole body seemed to be on fire.

Uncle Jim held out his hand. 'Give me the gun, Robert,' he said.

'Just try and take it off me,' I said.

Uncle Jim didn't move. He let his hand drop.

'Christ,' he said. 'Robert, do you really think I'd murder my own sister and brother-in-law? Mmm, do you? Two of the people I loved most in the whole world?'

I really didn't know what to believe any more.

'How can you explain this, then, eh?' I demanded, holding up the thimble again. 'And all the rest of my parents' stuff that I found in your loft. How can you explain that?'

'It's not the way it looks, Robert. I know how it must

94

look to you, but it's not like that. Why don't you put the gun down and let me explain?'

'Explain,' I said. 'I'll keep the gun.'

'Your father gave those things to me on the day he and your mother – my sister – were killed. He brought them over that morning and asked me to look after them. He said he was afraid something might happen to them.'

'What do you mean? What did he think was going to happen to them?'

'I honestly don't know. He was very vague. He just said he was worried about some of the valuable objects he had in the house. He wanted me to look after them. He must have thought they were in danger for some reason.'

'So that's why he had the gun, then,' I said, thinking aloud.

'Gun?' Uncle Jim repeated. 'What gun?'

The expression on his face had changed from shock to worry. It was strange, he actually looked more frightened now than when I'd first confronted him. My suspicions grew again.

'Didn't Dad tell you he'd bought a gun?' I said sharply. 'A revolver. Just a few days before he and Mum were killed. The police think it was probably the murder weapon.'

'Your dad never said anything to me about a gun.

Honestly, Robert, I swear to you,' Uncle Jim said. 'Did the police say whether they'd found it?'

'No, they haven't,' I said. 'And Donnelly doesn't reckon they ever will.'

The tension in Uncle Jim's face seemed to ease a little – but I held the gun tight still, aimed at his chest. I wasn't satisfied, yet.

'Why didn't you tell me all of this before?' I asked.

Uncle Jim shook his head. 'I should have done, I know,' he said. 'But you were in such a bad way after it happened, Robert. It was just about impossible to talk to you about anything.'

That was true enough, I had to admit. But there was still something wrong about his explanation. Something glaringly wrong.

'But what about that list you made for the police?' I asked. 'You knew those things weren't stolen, because they were in your loft all the time. Why did you tell the police they were?'

'I . . . Uh . . . I . . .' Uncle Jim hesitated. He raised his right hand and ran it hard through his greying, wiry hair.

'The truth is, Robert, I've been a bit of a fool,' he said. 'Of course I should have told the police those things were in my loft. I just thought that if they believed the theft of valuable items was involved in the case, then, well, maybe they'd get off their butts and do something about finding the vermin responsible for your parents' murder a bit quicker. That's all. I don't have a very high opinion of our police force, as you know. They seem to be much more interested in property than people's lives most of the time. I thought a Ming vase might just galvanize them into action . . . it doesn't seem to have worked though, does it?'

He looked at me rather sheepishly. And I stared back. For a few moments, neither of us moved. Then slowly I let my hand – the one holding the pistol – drop to my side. A sudden sense of relief rushed through me: I believed him. Thank God. It was terrible enough being parentless – to have found out the person responsible for their deaths was my closest surviving relative would just about have been the end.

'Chief Inspector Donnelly's too busy hoping to actually do anything,' I said. 'If we left him to it, we'd all be dead before we saw any results.'

'He's not exactly dynamic, is he?' Uncle Jim agreed.

Then he smiled. A very rueful smile.

'Now,' he said, 'how about you give me that air pistol before it goes off and breaks a window or something – and then I get us both a drink. You look like you could do with one. And I *certainly* could after the shock you gave me. Christ, Robert, you nearly frightened me to death, creeping up on me like that.'

He held his hand out for the gun. But instead of giving it to him, I took a step back away from him.

'No,' I said. 'I need it. I'll bring it back later, Uncle Jim, I promise. But I've got to have it this afternoon.'

'What do you mean you've got to have it this afternoon? Why have you got to have it this afternoon? Are you in some kind of trouble, Robert? It's not those thugs again, is it? Because if it is I—'

I interrupted him. 'No,' I said. 'It's not. It's something else I've got to sort out. Something to do with Dad.'

'Something to do with your dad?'

'Yes. But I haven't got time to explain now, Uncle Jim. I've got to meet someone. I'll talk to you about it later.'

Uncle Jim frowned. 'No, Robert,' he said, pointing at me. 'You'll talk to me about it right now. I'm your legal guardian now. I've got a right to know what you're doing. You can't just waltz out of here armed with an air pistol and say you'll explain it all later. Christ, Robert, what's going on?'

I glanced quickly at the kitchen clock. It was already gone eleven. It would take me a good hour to get to my rendezvous with Gerald. I couldn't afford to waste any more time.

'I'm sorry, Uncle Jim,' I said, turning towards the door, 'I haven't got time to explain now. I really haven't. I've got to go. What I'm doing is for Mum and Dad. For all of us. I'll see you later.'

I started to go out through the doorway.

'Robert!' Uncle Jim shouted, and he lunged forward and tried to grab me. But I was too quick for him. I sprinted along the hallway and pulled open the front door. I grabbed *Thérèse Raquin* and ran out into the drive, past Uncle Jim's car. I knew he must be close behind me and I was starting to panic. But then I had a stroke of luck. As I reached the end of the driveway, Aunty Susan's car turned into it from the road. She almost ran me down, in fact. I just leapt clear in time. I turned round just long enough to see that her car had pulled in alongside Uncle Jim's, blocking his path.

Then I ran like hell.

The train journey to London gave me some time to consider the implications of what I'd just discovered. In the space of half an hour I'd gone through the agony of convicting Uncle Jim and then the enormous relief of acquitting him of my parents' murder. And I'd learnt for sure that robbery wasn't the motive (at least not the usual kind of robbery). Which meant that, putting aside the extremely remote possibility some passing psychopath had been responsible, what it had to be about was those 'highly confidential' papers that Gerald had talked about. I looked at the book on my lap. Could this really be the key to the mystery? Or was it just another red herring? If it was, then Gerald wasn't going to be too happy. He was expecting the return of his precious papers – not some old French novel.

My mind went back to the lunch I'd had with Gerald (was it really only four days ago?) and that strange look I'd seen on his face when he'd started to talk about Dad and the missing documents. That look of severity – of accusation. His words hadn't accused me of anything – he'd even enlisted my help – but there was something about his look that had made me feel like I was an accomplice to some crime.

There was definitely more to this business of the documents than Gerald had so far let on. But what was it that he was concealing? And then there was the business of Dad and the gun. That had to fit in somewhere, surely. Uncle Jim had said that someone was threatening him. But who? Someone who wanted the documents? If so, then there must be more to them than Gerald had suggested. And what about the thugs who'd broken into the house the night before? Had Gerald sent them to get the documents? If so, then what I was doing now was extremely dangerous.

The thing was, though, I had no more choice in the matter than the train I was travelling in had in deciding its destination. I had to go on. I couldn't carry on living, knowing that I'd turned my back on finding out who had murdered my parents and why. I had to keep my appointment with Gerald just as surely as the train had to arrive at Victoria . . .

UKA's office is in a side street off Tottenham Court Road. In fact, it takes up just about the whole of the street. It's one of these very modern buildings – all glass and metal, like a giant mirror. Standing in front of it I felt very small. I put my hand on the air pistol where it was tucked in my belt under my zipper jacket. It made me feel a little more confident – David facing Goliath.

I announced myself to the security guard on the door. He rang up and got the all clear – from Gerald, presumably.

'Fifth floor. Turn left. Room 508,' said the guard abruptly, waving his arm in the direction of the lifts. Then he turned his attention back to his newspaper again.

I took the lift to the fourth floor. It was just a token precaution, but I didn't like the idea of walking straight out of the lift and into a hostile reception that I couldn't escape from. I walked up the flight of stairs to the fifth floor. Before I opened the door into the corridor, I peeked through the little window to make sure there was no one waiting to pounce on me. There wasn't. I started to think that maybe I was being unnecessarily paranoid. My palms were sweaty and I wiped them on my jeans before going out into the corridor.

I was very quiet. The only sound was the drone of a vacuum cleaner from the floor above. 'Turn left,' the guard had said. So I did. I walked slowly and softly along the corridor, looking at the numbers on the doors as I went. Room 508 was right down the end. I listened at the door for a moment – but I couldn't hear anything. I knocked. I heard the shuffle of a chair on carpet and then Gerald's voice, welcoming, suave: 'Come in, Robert.' I opened the door.

Gerald Finch was standing in front of his desk, smiling. He was more casually dressed than he'd been in the restaurant. In a white open-neck shirt and brown corduroy trousers, rather than smart grey suit and tie, he looked less severe – more like a father than a schoolmaster.

'It's good to see you,' he said, and gripped my hand firmly, the way he had before.

Despite my apprehensions and suspicions, the warmth of his greeting almost took me in. It was easy to see how he'd got where he had.

'That's a nasty bruise you've got there,' he said, looking at my eye. 'Has your doctor seen it?'

'It's OK,' I said. 'Just a bit of a black eye, that's all.'

'Nasty,' he said. 'Very nasty.'

He frowned sympathetically, his heavy brows forming a *V*. Then he smiled again.

'How about some coffee?' he asked. 'Or tea?'

'Coffee, please,' I said, then changed my mind. 'No, nothing, thanks.'

'It's no trouble,' he said persuasively. 'I was just going to get myself a cup anyway.'

But I declined again. Like I'd declined his offer of a car. I didn't want to be distracted from my purpose. I didn't want to feel even the slightest obligation towards Gerald. Because I knew things were going to get tough – and when they did, I'd have to be tough too.

While Gerald went to get a cup of coffee, I looked around his office. It was pretty much like Dad's had been – only much tidier. There were two rows of locked filing cabinets and a set of shelves neatly packed with books – in alphabetical order. The desk too was very orderly. There were none of the knick-knacks which you usually expect to see in people's offices. The only 'persona' object was a photograph of a boy, about my age. He was sitting on a gleaming motorcycle and he had a big, slightly smarmy grin. The resemblance to Gerald was unmistakable. Behind the desk a huge plate-glass window looked out over the West End. Oxford Street and Tottenham Court Road were a mass of people. Over to my right the British Telecom Tower stood straight and very tall, like a rocket waiting to be launched.

'Quite a view, isn't it?' said Gerald, coming back into the room.

'Yes,' I said, turning round. He had two cups in his hand.

'I know you said you didn't want one,' he said, 'but I brought one, just in case you changed your mind. Don't feel you have to drink it.'

He put one cup down at the front of the desk, then carried the other one round the other side to where his chair was. I noticed there was a large coffee stain on his shirt sleeve.

'Please, sit down,' he said, gesturing to the chair opposite.

I went and sat down. Gerald took a sip of his coffee. I didn't touch mine.

'Is that your son?' I asked, pointing to the photograph.

'Yes,' he said, proudly. 'Gordon. He's . . . How old are you?'

'Sixteen,' I said.

'Gordon's two years older. Eighteen. He's studying for his A levels at the moment. He should do very well, his teachers tell me. But then I don't suppose they know about the girlfriend or the motorbike. Both very time-consuming hobbies, I'm afraid.'

He looked at the photograph and smiled indulgently – a little too indulgently it seemed to me. As though he were overdoing the paternal bit to try and impress me. Then, still smiling, he looked at me.

'Well, Robert,' he said, 'I believe you have something for me.'

'Yes,' I said. 'I do.' I paused for a moment. 'But there are a few questions I'd like to ask you first.'

Gerald's smile faded and his heavy eyebrows started

to form themselves into a *V* again. He looked a little uneasy.

'Well, I'm not quite sure how I can help you, Robert, but by all means ask away . . .'

I gave him the straightest man-to-man stare I could ·manage.

'Before I ask,' I said, 'I'd like to tell you what's happened to me over the last few days. It might help you to answer my questions.'

I told Gerald about the burglary and about my search the following day (except I didn't say exactly what it was I'd found), and about the gun and what Uncle Jim had said about Dad being threatened – but not about the objects in the loft. All the time I spoke I watched Gerald's face very closely. The deep lines formed patterns of surprise and concern – but I saw no guilt in his eyes.

'So you see,' I said, 'Mum and Dad weren't killed for their valuable possessions. I think they were murdered because of those highly confidential documents you told me about . . .' I paused and took a deep breath. 'I also suspect that you sent those thugs the other night to get those documents back – just in case I didn't come up with them. Or maybe to scare me into putting a bit more urgency into my search . . .'

Gerald raised his hands in protest.

'No, Robert, no,' he said. 'Whatever put that idea in

your head? I'm on your side. I asked for your assistance. I'm absolutely appalled by what happened to you the other night. It's terrible. Shocking. Believe me.'

'Well, who was responsible then?' I asked.

'I don't know. But I assure you, Robert, it had nothing to do with me – or UKA. Absolutely not.'

I leant forward slightly in my chair, feeling the gun, like some sort of lucky talisman, under my jacket. I decided it was time to go for the jugular.

'Look,' I said. 'I know I'm only seventeen years old. But I'm not an idiot . . . The other day, when we had lunch, you told me about those papers and yet, yesterday, when Chief Inspector Donnelly came to see you, you denied any knowledge of them and suggested to him that I'd imagined the whole thing because I'd been drunk or emotionally unstable or some such rubbish. Before I give you any papers, I want to know what's going on . . . I've got a right to know.'

Gerald and I were eyeball to eyeball now across the desk. I could tell that he'd been taken aback by the directness of my approach. He probably hadn't counted on my discovering as much as I had. For an instant we just sat there motionless, as though we were playing that kids' staring-out game, waiting to see who would blink first. Then he sighed, got up from his chair and walked over to the window. He looked out for a moment with his back to me. When he turned, he'd let the suave charm drop a little. The expression on his face was more severe; he was Gerald the bird man again, which, I hoped, might mean I'd get a few straight answers.

'You have got those documents, Robert, haven't you?' he asked.

I patted the chest of my jacket.

'Right here,' I said.

'You're placing me in an extremely awkward position,' he said. 'Because, while I agree that morally you have every right to know what this is all about – in so far as it concerns your father – as far as the company's concerned, you have no right at all. And it's far too delicate a matter to let the police get involved. I'm sorry if I made you seem foolish in the eyes of Chief Inspector Donnelly, but I did stress to you that the matter was highly confidential. This is an issue of national security. It goes far beyond UKA. I didn't expect you to go and reveal what I'd told you to the police. This isn't a police matter, Robert. This is government business – and the powers that be want this whole thing kept under wraps. Do you understand?'

'I want to know,' I said stubbornly.

'Yes,' he said, nodding. 'You are very like your father. I only hope, though, Robert, that there are some aspects of his personality that you have not inherited . . .'

He let this thinly veiled accusation float in the air — maybe to test my reaction; to see how much I knew. I kept him in suspense for a moment or two, before speaking. Then I said, 'Dad took those papers, didn't he?'

Gerald picked up his glasses from the desk and twiddled them a couple of times. Then he looked at me.

'Yes,' he said. 'Yes, Robert, I am afraid he did. And, to be quite frank, he really dropped us in the shit.'

From the lips of the suave, polite, mealy-mouthed Gerald, the four-letter word had the force of an explosion — full of bitterness, resentment and accusation. It knocked me back a little. I felt uncomfortable — guilty.

'There are a few things, Robert, that you ought to know about your father,' Gerald continued. 'Things that you might not like. I hoped that I wouldn't have to tell you about them. But, now, I don't seem to have much choice, do I? You say you want to know — so, know . . . you . . . shall.' He waved his glasses at me, by way of punctuation.

I didn't say anything. This is what I'd come to hear, but I had a feeling that Gerald was right — that I wasn't going to enjoy hearing it. Gerald started to pace up and down in front of the window. It made him look more than ever like a bird. A giant bird of prey.

'In the restaurant the other day I said that your father was quite a joker, didn't I? Well, he was. He had a wonderful sense of humour – how we all laughed. Until we realized that he'd been saving his biggest and nastiest joke to play on us, his friends and colleagues. I knew your father for twelve years – *twelve years*. I liked him. I thought we were friends, and yet he betrayed our friendship and his company, just like that. For money. Like Judas. I suppose they offered him lots of money – he liked his comforts . . . And then, of course, there was that woman. I imagine – knowing your father – that she had something to do with it.'

'What woman?' I said. But Gerald ignored my question. He carried on, almost ranting now.

'You might call it industrial espionage – I suppose he would have done. But to me it was treachery. He stole documents vital to the success of a project which was going to help put this country back on its feet. Provide jobs, prestige, a great future for UKA . . .'

'So you killed him,' I said, getting up out of my chair. My head was throbbing with fury. 'You had him killed, right?' I spoke without thinking, as if my tongue had a mind of its own.

Things were going faster than I'd expected. I felt hot. I felt like I was on the edge of some horrible fiery chasm – about to be sucked down into its flames.

Gerald raised his hands. He looked shocked.

'No, Robert,' he said. 'No, I didn't kill him. Nor did I

have him killed. I had every reason to hate him. But this is a business, not the Mafia. We don't go round killing people. I can only suppose *they* did it – his so-called chums. Quite an irony that . . . The betrayer betrayed. The final sordid joke was on the arch joker himself. Well, no one can say he didn't deserve what he got.'

I looked at Gerald in horror.

'You're talking about my father,' I said. 'Sod your bloody betrayals. Sod your bloody documents and your jokes. How would you feel if someone had murdered your precious bloody Gordon? My mum and dad are dead, murdered. And you know who did it. So tell me. I want to know. I want to know, now.'

As I spoke, I put my hand inside my jacket and pulled out the air pistol. I waved it at Gerald.

'I want to know everything,' I said.

The look on Gerald's face changed from anger to fear. I could tell the gun had obviously unnerved him. He tried to say something, but couldn't get the words out. It was strange the way fear overwhelmed him so quickly and so totally. All trace of suavity had gone. I suddenly felt powerful – like in a childish game of pretending, where you make your own rules.

'All right,' he spluttered, 'all right.'

He sat down heavily in his chair.

'I'll tell you. If you really want to know, I'll tell you . . .'

111

He put his head in his hands.

'I'll tell you,' he said again, very quietly, like all the energy had gone out of him.

He told me about Dad and the papers – the whole story. Or as much as he knew of it, anyway. He said again that for the last couple of years Dad had been working on this really important project, developing some special kind of foil that would revolutionize the market. The new foil, apparently, had potential defence applications that had attracted the interest and support of the government. They'd virtually taken over the project. Everything had gone smoothly for the first year and a half, but then suspicions started to arise that highly confidential project information was being leaked to a competitor. Documents went temporarily missing and then turned up again mysteriously in the place where everyone had looked for them. Things like that. What led them to Dad was a chance spotting of him and a couple of employees from UKA's French competitor at a stamp market one Sunday, off the Champs Élysées in Paris. They seemed to be deep in conversation. Which got people wondering about Dad and his French trips. If anyone was leaking information, he certainly had the greatest opportunity. No one wanted to believe it, though – Dad was so highly thought of. He'd done so much for the company. But they had him watched all the same. And in the end he slipped up. He took home some documents that should under no circumstances have left the office. But even then he bluffed his way out of it. He said that he'd thought the team was on the edge of a crucial breakthrough and he'd been afraid to leave the documents in the office – in case they should be taken. He'd thought they'd be safer with him, at home, just for one night – until security in the office could be assured. And because he was who he was they'd accepted his explanation, eventually. But apparently some strong threats had been made to Dad 'from on high', as Gerald put it, about what would happen to any 'traitor'. It was after that, I suppose, that Dad bought the revolver.

Gerald reckoned that UKA's French competitors had been responsible for Mum and Dad's murder. Important documents had been taken from the office the night before and Dad had been the only one who could have taken them. When the theft had been discovered the next morning, Dad couldn't be found. The evidence pointed to him so strongly, though, that it seemed clear he was about to make the final deal and get his payoff – before leaving the country, probably. Gerald's view was that Dad had got too greedy – tried to hold the French to ransom – and so they killed him. Mum was just unlucky enough to be around when they did it. The robbery, he said, was just a smoke screen. It had been a perfect crime. Except, of course, they hadn't got the documents, because I had them – or so I'd led Gerald to believe.

Gerald's voice was little more than a tired mumble now. Sitting forward in his chair, his arm on the desk, supporting his head, he looked rather pathetic. Without his smooth façade and with his ranting spent, he was a picture of a man under terrible strain. He reminded me of a teacher I'd had once, whose wife had died. It went against the grain, though, to feel sorry for teachers – just as it went against the grain to feel sorry for the man who'd said such hard things about your dead father. I had to be strong if I was ever going to get to the bottom of this business – and *I had to*, because no one else would. Not the great hoper Donnelly, I thought, that was for sure.

'So, Robert, what now?' Gerald said quietly. 'Have you heard enough? Can I have the documents now?'

He looked at his watch.

'I have a lunch appointment in twenty minutes . . .'

'I've got one more question,' I said, and I put my hand in my jacket pocket and took out the photograph of the woman that I'd found in the book. 'You said something about a woman. Is this her?' I handed Gerald the picture.

Gerald's eyebrows formed themselves into a heavy *V* once more.

'Madame Calimet,' he said. 'That's the woman all right.'

'What did she have to do with all this then?' I asked.

'She was David's – your father's – contact. She worked for one of UKA's biggest European customers at one time – until she joined our rivals Aluminium Français. She was almost certainly the one who persuaded your father to sell our secrets. They were seen together on quite a few occasions – at the stamp market . . . and elsewhere.'

My throat felt dry. There was a question forming to which I didn't know if I wanted to learn the answer. But I had to ask.

'Was Dad having an affair with her?' I asked.

'How should I know?' said Gerald wearily. 'Ask her. Ask Madame Calimet. I don't know what sordid practices your father indulged in in his private life. They were very close, that's all I know.'

'But if they were close, why would she have Dad murdered?'

Gerald gave a snort of disdain.

'Madame Calimet is not the sort of woman to let *les sentiments* get in the way of her business ambitions. Judging by her track record so far, there's not a lot that woman wouldn't do to further her career. She'll probably be a minister one day.'

I looked at the photograph and was struck once more by the face's strangely mocking expression. She was a very attractive woman, but her green eyes, though enticing, were rather cold and hard, like the emeralds around her neck. She looked sort of devious – the exact opposite of Mum. I felt somehow that it would be a lot more difficult confronting Madame Calimet than it had been Gerald or Uncle Jim. She looked like she'd eat me alive.

'Where can I find her?' I asked.

Gerald looked at me, shaking his head.

'You don't seriously believe, Robert, do you, that you can just wander round the Continent threatening people until they tell you what you want to know? Do you? Leave all that to the proper authorities . . . Now, I need those documents.'

'First,' I said, 'I have to know where to find her.'

'I don't know where she lives,' Gerald said, getting irritable now. 'All I know is that she met your father regularly at the stamp market off the Champs Élysées. She goes there every Sunday morning. It's one of her little rituals. Now, please, I have a lunch appointment and I need those documents.'

Gerald no longer seemed afraid. I had the feeling he was getting desperate now, which wasn't good news. Because if it came down to a struggle, I wasn't at all sure that I'd come off best. I took the book out of my jacket.

'I haven't actually got any documents,' I said. 'I found this book.'

'A book?'

'Yes. It's a French novel – *Thérèse Raquin*. It was hidden away in a secret cupboard. I thought maybe it contained some kind of code.'

'Let me see.'

I handed Gerald the book. He put on his glasses and flicked through it. Then he took off his glasses again.

'Is this some kind of joke, Robert?' he said. 'Because if it is, you are playing a very silly, very dangerous game.'

'I know it's important,' I said. 'Why else would Dad have hidden it so carefully?'

'It's a book, Robert. A French novel. I asked you to look for documents. Very important, highly confidential documents. I know they were in your house somewhere – so where are they?'

He waved the book at me like a weapon.

'Don't play bloody infantile games with me now, Robert.' His voice was raised, menacing.

'I'm not playing games,' I said fiercely, grabbing the book back as I did so. Gerald held on, though, and the cover started to tear away from the spine. I wrestled with him for a moment before snatching it from his grasp. I stood up and raised the gun again. Gerald stood up too and started to move round the desk.

'Stand back,' I said. 'Don't come any closer. I'm going to keep this book. I know it's got something to do with all this.' And then, suddenly, something dawned on me.

'You keep going on about these documents, but how do I know they really exist? Maybe it's something else you're after. Something of Dad's. Something you'd killed him to get your hands on. Or maybe these documents don't belong to you at all. Maybe they belong to the French and *you're* trying to steal them . . .'

'I'm tired of all this, Robert,' Gerald said menacingly. 'I want those documents.'

He started to move towards me.

'I'm warning you,' I said. 'Don't come any nearer.'

But he did. And I knew I'd have to fire a shot and that it would have to make one hell of an impact, because the pistol only held one pellet and I wouldn't have time to reload. And then my gaze fell on the photograph. I stepped to my right so that it and Gerald and I were almost in a line. Then as Gerald came nearer, I fired. Gerald must have seen my finger tighten on the trigger, because he cowered and went down on his knees. As he did so, there was a tinkling of breaking glass and the photograph of Gordon fell down behind the desk.

Ignoring me, Gerald crawled over to where the smashed photograph lay on the floor. He was whimpering.

'Gordon,' he said, 'Gordon,' as though I'd actually shot Gordon himself – not just a photograph of him. I

froze for a moment, astonished by what I was seeing –
but then, with an unusually quick bit of thinking, I took
advantage of Gerald's disarray to pull out the telephone
cable from the socket. It seemed the only chance I had of
getting out of the building before Gerald alerted the
security guard. I grabbed the telephone and made
quickly for the door. Outside I wound the end of the cable
tightly round the door handle and did the same with the
flex from the receiver round the door handle opposite, so
that a taut wire stretched across the corridor, with the
telephone itself dangling rather absurdly between. It
probably wouldn't hold Gerald back for long, once he'd
recovered his composure – but hopefully it would delay
any alarm just long enough for me to make my escape.

I tore down the staircase, falling down one flight and
almost breaking my neck in the process. It seemed to
take me ages to get to the bottom – though I suppose it
was no more than a couple of minutes. Surely, I thought,
Gerald would have alerted the guard by now. I took a
couple of deep breaths before going out into the lobby, to
try and appear a bit more normal. But I could feel my
heart hammering and my stomach felt sick as I walked
towards the front door. The guard didn't turn round till I
reached him, so I couldn't see until the very last minute
whether he knew or not . . .

He didn't.

'Meeting over?' he said, looking up without interest over his newspaper.

'Yes,' I said, trying to smile naturally.

Slowly, very slowly, he put down his newspaper, got up and walked over to the door. He jangled his keys, looking for the one he needed, then unlocked the door and, finally, opened it. I thought I was going to explode. It was like being subjected to the Chinese water torture. Every moment I expected to hear some kind of alarm go off or Gerald's voice calling for me to be apprehended.

The security guard stood by the door, holding it, waiting for me to go past.

'Thanks,' I said, walking out into the street. He nodded and then closed the door after me. I heard the keys jangle again as he locked up.

I'd escaped. I was free. I didn't dare look back. I walked a few steps, then I sprinted off down the street.

I don't know if I want to go on with this. It's turning into some kind of thriller. A real bloody ripping yarn. But what happens at the end of it? After the credits roll, or the last page has been turned? What sort of life is there left for me? Even if this whole lousy thing finally gets cleared up, what good will it really do me? I'll still be an orphan, won't I? And Mum and Dad will still be dead . . .

I said to Sigmund, 'I'm not going to go through all this just for your bloody satisfaction, just so that you can tick me off in your book of case histories and collect your fee. I want to know what's going to happen to me.'

Sigmund said that he understood my anxieties – that they were only natural. But as to satisfaction, that could only come from me. He could neither provide nor receive it, unless I had done so first. It really was up to me.

I got annoyed. I said that was typical. That was a typical adult reaction. Make you do all the work. Make you sort out all their bloody mess. Throw all the responsibility and blame back on you. And then sit back and criticize. I'm tired of all this double-dealing, game-playing, cloak-and-dagger crap. I'm tired of Sigmund too . . . He really pisses me off.

Uncle Jim came to the clinic this afternoon. But I wouldn't see him. He left me a letter. One of the nurses gave it to me. I screwed it up and chucked it out into the corridor. Then I lay on my bed for hours, thinking, cursing, feeling terrible, I dropped off for a little while and dreamt that Mum came in and ran her cool, elegant hands soothingly over my forehead and through my hair – the way she used to do when I was younger. I woke up feeling wonderful and optimistic, but then I remembered the actual state of things and felt worse than ever. Stone-cold desolate. Inconsolable. Like I'd been weighed down with concrete and dropped into a river of despair.

At least when I'm writing, I suppose, I'm spared all that for a while.

After leaving the UKA offices, I phoned Uncle Jim. I needed my passport and money and I couldn't risk going back home myself to get them. Gerald might have called the police, and home was the first place they'd go to find me. Uncle Jim wasn't at all happy about helping me. He wanted me to go back to his place right away and sort things out from there. But it had all gone too far now for turning back. I had to get to Paris. I had to bully and threaten Uncle Jim, mentioning the stuff in his attic, to get him to agree to assist me. It was blackmail really and I didn't like doing it, but I was determined to see this thing through, whatever it took. He said he'd meet me at Victoria station in an hour.

I killed the time checking on trains and then sitting in one of the many cheap pizza places that surround the station. I ordered a pizza, but when it came I hardly touched it. My adrenalin was pumping too quickly even for the fastest of fast food. I wanted to be on my way.

Around me people with rucksacks chatted happily in the brightly lit phoney Alpine décor. It was just the kind of place, I thought grimly, that Dad wouldn't have been seen dead in.

Uncle Jim arrived just late enough for me to start worrying whether he'd thought better of helping me out. I was very relieved to see him. He said that he and Aunty Susan had been very concerned about me, then he gave me the expected haranguing about not keeping him properly informed and about doing things that were better left to the police – which I thought was a bit rich, considering his opinion of them. Apparently Donnelly had been looking for me. He wouldn't tell Uncle Jim why. It was something important, he'd said, which made me wonder whether all his hoping was finally getting him somewhere. I had no time to waste finding out, though. I tried to play down to Uncle Jim the danger in what I was doing and play up its importance in finding out the truth. I'd be careful, I said. Uncle Jim wasn't at all convinced, I could tell – and he kept trying to persuade me to go back with him. But I wasn't going to give in and, in the end, reluctantly, he handed me a zipper bag with my passport and the money I'd asked for, and a few other things he'd packed for me as well. In return, I gave him back his air pistol wrapped in a plastic carrier.

There was an awkward silence while I put the book

into the bag and I could sense Uncle Jim's unease. He looked very tired too and I felt sorry for him. It struck me suddenly just how much he and Aunty Susan must have gone through over the past few days – and months before that.

'You've got something to read on the journey then,' he said quietly, just for something to say, I suppose.

'Oh, yes. Just some old book I picked up off the shelves at home,' I lied uncomfortably. I fiddled with the zip on the bag and tried to cover my discomfort.

'I'll bring you back a French tart,' I joked, feebly.

Uncle Jim didn't smile.

'Just bring yourself back . . . in one piece,' he said gravely. Then he added, 'Sometimes, you know, Robert, it's better to let sleeping dogs lie. Remember that.'

'But not if they're barking up the wrong tree,' I said, thinking of Donnelly and his robbers – then wished I hadn't because it sounded so flip and silly.

'I'd better get my ticket,' I said, embarrassed.

A few minutes later, I was ready to go.

'For Christ's sake, Robert, take care of yourself,' was Uncle Jim's parting comment, as I passed through the barrier to the platform. I turned round when I reached the train and saw him still standing there, with a look of real concern on his face. And I felt a pang of guilt, because I was still naive enough to think he was concerned about me.

The train journey down to the coast gave me plenty of time to worry about how I was going to get through customs if Gerald had alerted the police. I had a feeling that a youth, travelling on his own – especially one with a dirty great black eye – would be an ideal target for one of those hawk-eyed plain-clothes police you get hovering around the passport-control desks. I tried to think up a convincing story to tell them if they asked me why I was going to France, where I was going to stay or what I was going to do there. I decided in the end that I'd say I was going youth hostelling, because it sounded sort of wholesome.

As it happened, though, I didn't get stopped. There were a couple of guys in front of me weighed down with rucksacks and stuff – and they got stopped. A quick glance and nod from the passport officer and I was on my way to the boat.

The ferry was pretty crowded. Dad hated crowds, especially ferry crowds – he said they had the beer-swilling football-fan mentality – but today's crowd didn't worry me. After changing some money at the bureau de change window, I spent most of the crossing on deck. It was dark, but there was surprisingly little wind for the time of year, and it wasn't too cold. Sitting there in the gloom, between two shores, with my jacket wrapped around me and my zipper bag by my side, I felt strangely elated. Like I was going into some great adventure – a voyage of discovery. It was the first time I'd ever travelled abroad on my own. I thought of those geography students in that Longhi painting – particularly the elegant woman at the centre. She sat with her hands on a globe, looking out and, it seemed, exhorting me to go on and accomplish my mission. And then I realized the face I was seeing was Mum's face – that lovely, warm, expressive face – which made the exhortation that much stronger and more poignant, because, if I was doing all this for anyone, it should be for Mum. After all, she was the only truly innocent victim in all this, wasn't she?

The platform clock at Calais station was showing ten past eight when I boarded the train for Paris. The first thing I did when I found my seat was to wind my watch forward. It felt a bit odd, just tossing an hour away like that, but it felt good too, because that was one less hour for me to fill before the morning and my meeting – hopefully – with Madame Calimet.

The train was quite empty, so I had space to spread myself a little and get comfortable. I was on the verge of dozing off, in fact, when the ticket collector came round demanding *billets*. After that I didn't feel sleepy at all. I *did* feel hungry though. Uncle Jim had said he'd put a bit of food in the bag he'd given me and I felt in real need of it now. I'd hardly eaten a thing all day – and it had been quite some day. I unzipped the bag and had a root around. I found some fruit and a couple of rounds of home-made sandwiches – foil-wrapped, of course. There was a can of lager too. I took it all out and put it on the table in front of me.

While I devoured my little feast, I thought back over the events of the day . . . So much had happened that it seemed like days ago that I'd set out from home *en route* for Uncle Jim's to get the air pistol. Then there'd been the search of the loft and the discovery of my parents' stuff, my angry confrontation with Uncle Jim, his explanations, my hurried escape and then Gerald. I still didn't know quite what to make of my meeting with Gerald. All that stuff about government involvement, the 'powers that be' et cetera – was he just trying to scare me?

I decided to have another look at *Thérèse Raquin*. The first thing I noticed on opening the book was how loose the front cover had become. It sort of flapped, where it had torn from its binding. I suppose that must have happened in my struggle with Gerald. And then I noticed that a corner of the sticker on the inside of the cover was curled up where it had come unstuck from the book. Closer inspection revealed what I should have thought of some time before – as soon as Aunty Barbara told me about the 'new' cover and the fake sticker: there was something else other than the inside of the cover concealed beneath the sticker. A triangle of white paper peeped out from beneath the curled corner.

Carefully, I peeled back the rest of the sticker and pulled out the sheet of paper that lay under it. A rectangular hollow had been neatly cut out of the book's chunky cover, making a hidey-hole like the one Dad had carved in the back of my cupboard. In the hollow, wrapped in cotton wool like a piece of jewellery, was a small roll of film. Unpleasant thoughts were already beginning to form in my head when I found the piece of paper at the bottom of the hollow. The writing on it was Dad's. It read: *Voici la seule copie qui reste. Les originaux ont été détruits comme prévu.*

My French was no great shakes, but it didn't have to be to understand pretty quickly what the message signified. It meant that Gerald had been telling the truth about the documents: they really did exist – and Dad had taken them. He'd copied and then destroyed them. The house of cards I'd started building during my meeting with Gerald – that Dad was the wronged one, that Dad was a victim – came tumbling down around me. What Gerald had said was true – Dad was a 'traitor', involved in industrial espionage, and because of it, and those bloody secret documents, he and Mum had been killed. Gerald's words at the restaurant about Dad making a good spy came back to me. The idea had sounded quite appealing then; now, no longer an idea but the cause of my parents' murder, it was appalling.

As the train whooshed through the darkness, I suddenly felt terribly lonely and vulnerable and young. The carriage I was in was full of adults, with their newspapers and briefcases, speaking a foreign tongue, and I felt excluded – as much by my age as by my foreignness. I felt oppressed by the sheer size and weight of this heavy grown-up world of expectations, responsibilities, revelations. I was an ant trying to do the job of Atlas. And it didn't look like the load would ever get any lighter. Inside my head, too, adult faces crowded – Mum, Dad, Uncle Jim, Donnelly, the woman in the photo, Gerald . . . Gerald especially. I'd tried to hate him, blame him, accuse him – because he seemed to be doing the same to Dad. But now I had to admit he had had a genuine cause.

I pictured Gerald as I'd last seen him, crawling on the floor picking up the shattered pieces of glass from his son's photograph. I thought about his casual dress and the coffee stain on his sleeve. I didn't like the picture one bit. Gerald smarmy, suave and strong I could cope with – but Gerald whimpering and weak I couldn't handle at all. I suppose it made me feel too guilty.

I looked at the book again, where it lay open on the table in front of me – and I recalled what Aunty Barbara had told me of the story of *Thérèse Raquin*. I hadn't realized then just how close a resemblance that sorry story had with my own – or Dad's anyway. A story of treachery, of murder . . . of adultery? Gerald hadn't said that Dad was having an affair with Madame Calimet, but he had sort of hinted at it. They were very close, he'd said. Thick as thieves, I thought bitterly. I remembered the photograph and took it out. There was that chic, mocking face looking at me. Was it the face of Dad's lover? Dad's murderer?

My mind turned again to the ordeal that lay ahead. I was pretty sure that getting answers out of her wasn't going to be easy. If she had been involved somehow in Mum and Dad's murder – and was as unscrupulous as Gerald had suggested – then she wasn't going to come out and confess to me, was she? There was no reason really why she should tell me anything at all. I'd have to keep my wits about me, that was for sure. And hope that nothing prevented her from taking her habitual Sunday walk to the stamp market, of course. The thought that she might not – after coming all this way, going through all I'd gone through – was just too terrible to contemplate. She just had to show up . . .

*   *   *

131

I spent the night in a little hotel near the Gare du Nord. The Arab desk clerk gave me some funny looks at first – but when he realized I was English his face broke out into a huge grin and he was suddenly very obliging. 'Is OK. Is good,' he said. The room was very small and pretty dingy, but it wasn't too expensive and it suited my purposes all right. All I needed was somewhere to lay my head.

The shutters on the street cafés were still closed when I left early the next morning. I'd been to Paris a couple of times before with Mum and Dad, but we'd spent our time in the more up-market parts round the Rue Saint-Honoré or the Champs Élysées – where I was headed now. In the early morning gloom, the streets round the Gare du Nord were rather shabby and grimy in comparison, but there was still something rather magical about them. Perhaps it was just that I was in Paris in the autumn. Dad's favourite time. 'Forget springtime, autumn's the best time to be in Paris,' he used to say. Then he'd start quoting Baudelaire: '*C'était hier l'été; voici l'automne!*' I don't know how many times I'd heard that line.

I found a map in the station which showed me how to get to the Avenue des Champs Élysées. It was a pretty long road and I didn't know exactly where on it I'd find the market, so I decided to start from the top, at the Arc de Triomphe, and work my way down. I got a ticket for the RER, which is this kind of superfast tube train which goes along a different line from the ordinary Métro. I got a little confused at first, because the French underground system uses destinations, rather than names of lines or compass directions, to indicate where you should go. In the end, though, I found the right platform for the RER train to Charles de Gaulle Étoile.

I was struck by how much cleaner, brighter and more high-tech the Paris Métro system seemed than the London Underground. The stink, though, on the journey itself was terrible – it was like we were going through sewage. I remembered something Dad had said about the RER being deeper down than the London Underground – nearer the sewers. Whatever the reason, I was pretty pleased when we finally reached Charles de Gaulle and I could get out into the relatively fresh air once more.

As I walked down the Champs Élysées, away from the magnificent Arc de Triomphe, the great glass-fronted cafés were just starting to show signs of opening. Smart waiters in white aprons turned chairs off tables. There was a smell of coffee and croissants in the air. Here and there, newspaper kiosks displayed their wares. But all in all, apart from the odd person walking his or her dog, there were very few people about. It was quite a contrast to London the day before . . .

As I reached some traffic lights, a tramp, stinking of

wine, staggered into me. '*Merde!*' he grumbled, then tottered on. But I stopped still, because that one word struck me like a revelation. I'd heard it before and very recently. Just the other night, in fact, the night of the attempted burglary. It hadn't been 'Ahmed' or any other name that my attacker had called out – it had been '*Ah, merde!*': shit. My attacker had been French. So I was on the right track.

Deep in thought, I walked on, down the Avenue. I didn't see any sign of a stamp market, but then I supposed I was probably too early. What did catch my eye, though, were the trees that lined the pavement. There was something rather grotesque about their bare, gnarled, heavily pruned branches. They looked like mutants, like victims of violence, forced to publicly parade their injuries. I found them pretty creepy – like a bad omen.

Finally, I came to some gardens – well, I say gardens, but really it was sections of raked sandy clay punctuated by more mutated trees and the occasional pond. It was a setting I soon recognized. I took out the photograph to make sure. I was standing in the Jardin des Tuileries. *Her* territory. Whoever she really was. I wondered if Dad had taken the photo; if so, then he would probably have been standing somewhere close to where I was standing now. Laughing maybe, saying something to make his subject smile. Alive. It might have been only a couple of months ago. And then, just a little while later, did his subject have *him* shot? Mum too? I turned and started to walk back the way I'd come.

This time I found the market – although it would have been pretty easy to miss. I suppose I was expecting to see a whole mass of stalls and stuff. Not the mere three that there actually were, set up on an edge of one of the Avenue's little squares – which were no more really than bits of dusty wasteland with a few trees and benches. I had a quick browse, just to establish myself as a potential customer so that I wouldn't look too suspicious hanging around, then I sat down on a bench a little way off where I had a clear view of what was going on at the market.

For quite a while, nothing much did go on. I sat on the bench or paced about, getting pretty cold and hungry. But I didn't dare go off and buy myself a cup of coffee and a croissant, in case Madame Calimet arrived while I was away. At least it wasn't raining, I thought. Rain would have been a disaster. In fact it was quite a pleasant autumn day. While I waited, I mulled over what I'd discovered about the break-in and what it meant – which was, basically, that Madame Calimet and her company had to have been responsible. It meant too that another of Gerald's assertions had been proved true. He had had nothing to do with it.

After a couple of hours or so, the atmosphere round the market started to liven up a bit. The arrival of browsers became more frequent, smartly dressed Parisians and brightly clad tourists passed by on the Avenue, church bells rang and a group of elderly men turned up to play boules on the waste ground behind where I was sitting. And then another group arrived. By eleven o'clock the place was really quite alive.

It was another hour or more, though, before anything happened that was of real interest to me. Just as I was starting to think I'd run myself into a cul-de-sac and was facing up gloomily to the idea that my quest was doomed to failure, a woman came walking towards the market from the Avenue off to my right. Dressed in a full-length red leather coat and with her bright peroxide-blonde hair, she stood out like a sore thumb. The moment I saw her, I felt the adrenalin pumping. My quest was alive once more. Madame Calimet had arrived.

She browsed around the stalls for a while, chatting for a few minutes with one of the stallholders – but she didn't seem particularly interested in the stamps. She kept glancing at her watch and then looking around the square, as though she were waiting for someone. A couple of times her eyes swept over me and I had a job holding my nerve and not betraying myself. I had to keep reminding myself that of course she didn't know me from

Adam. It was Dad she knew. His teenage son was probably the last person she was expecting to see – if, indeed, she even knew I existed.

I saw her reaction to the person she'd obviously been waiting for before I saw the man himself. It was a look of annoyance – obviously she hadn't liked being kept waiting. By the time he reached her, though, her face had formed itself into a smile and she met him with a greeting and a handshake that were ostentatiously friendly. Then they walked away together, over to a bench along from where I was sitting – on the same side of the square.

Once they sat down, I couldn't see either of them very well, because the man had his very considerable back to me, blocking her from my view almost entirely. Just about the only thing I could see clearly were her hands, which were constantly in motion. And even in those rare moments when they were still, they spoke volumes. Madame Calimet was obviously pretty tense and wound up about something. Whoever the man was, he wasn't the casual friendly acquaintance she'd tried to make out and the news he'd brought her wasn't exactly to her liking. I wondered if it had anything to do with Dad – or those bloody documents. The documents they still didn't have.

After about ten minutes of animated discussion, the hand-waving stopped suddenly and Madame Calimet got up and strode off, pulling the collar of her coat up around her neck. She seemed really uptight now. A moment later the man got up too. And in the split second he turned to half face me, I was certain I knew who he was. I'd only seen his face briefly before, but I was sure that the man I was looking at was the man who'd attacked me just a couple of nights before. I turned my back quickly, scared stiff that he might recognize me. I still had the bruises from our first encounter; I had no desire to collect any more. Or worse.

I started to walk away slowly across the square, in the general direction of Madame Calimet's moving form. Then, when I reached the side road she was walking down and I thought I'd put enough distance between myself and the man, I quickened my pace. I needed to as well, because by now Madame Calimet was almost at the corner of the street.

I wouldn't have figured Madame Calimet for a great walker – somehow taxis and limousines looked more in her line – but she certainly covered a lot of metres of pavement over the next twenty minutes or so. We probably didn't go much further than a mile and a half, but not knowing where I was going and having to con-centrate hard on keeping her in sight without giving myself away, it seemed twice as far. A couple of times I nearly lost her, once when she disappeared for a few moments into the large crowd outside a church and then when she popped into a pâtisserie and, not seeing her, I carried on walking. Luckily, it was only a fleeting stop, so that by the time I'd realized she wasn't ahead of me and started to look around in panic, she was back on the street again. I crossed the road and looked in a shop window until she was ahead of me, then I was off and following her once more.

Along main streets and down side roads we went – past I don't know how many of those gnarled, stunted trees – until finally Madame Calimet stopped at a gate entrance in an archway, beyond which I could see a small courtyard. I stood, just across the street, in a shop door-way, while she pressed out a combination number with a long, black-leather-gloved finger on a series of buttons by the gate. I'd known from previous trips to Paris how difficult it was to get into blocks of apartments like this one – there was nearly always some kind of lock on the entrance or else a concierge to get past – and that's why I'd taken the risk of getting so close now. It was my only chance of getting in and confronting Madame Calimet.

As she pulled the heavy door open, I started to move quickly but quietly across the road towards her, hoping that I'd have a few moments to catch the door before it clicked itself shut. Had it not been a self-closing door, of course, I wouldn't have stood a chance. As it was, I timed my movement perfectly, reaching the door just as the lock was about to engage. I put my hand on the door and pushed it open again . . . I was in. Ahead of me, the tapping of Madame Calimet's heels on the flagstones echoed noisily around the courtyard and then stopped suddenly when she disappeared through a door opposite where I was standing. There was a lightness, a kind of exhilaration, in my step as I crossed the courtyard after her, the rubber soles of my Doc Martens hardly making a sound. At last and against all the odds, the time of reckoning had come – and it was I alone who was responsible for bringing it about. I don't think I'd ever felt such a sense of achievement in my life before.

I went through the door and climbed up the carpeted staircase, listening for any sound of Madame Calimet above me. I heard the jangling then the knocking of keys as locks were released, and then I saw the open door itself and the back of Madame Calimet's blonde-headed, red-leathered figure poised to enter her apartment. But before she did I called out her name.

'Madame Calimet!'

She turned round quickly, the look on her made-up face more one of irritation than of curiosity.

'*Oui?*' she said sharply, questioningly.

It was the first time I'd seen her face to face, the first time I'd clearly heard her voice. And it threw me. For an instant I was completely tongue-tied. I didn't know what to say. It was she who spoke.

'*Qui êtes-vous?*' she asked.

And then it was easy. 'I'm Robert Harrison,' I said. 'David Harrison's son.'

Now it was her turn to be lost for words. For a very long moment neither of us moved or spoke. She stood there in the doorway, staring at me. Then she took a deep breath and shook her head.

'*Mon Dieu!*' she said.

Yesterday was a bad day. One of the worst. As soon as I walked into the room I knew things were going to be bad. I looked around at all those books on all those shelves and the bulging filing cabinets – all that knowledge – and I suddenly felt so frustrated, so angry because none of it was of any use to me. It was like being back at school again. And then Sigmund made it worse by giving me a volume of Baudelaire's verse, *Les Fleurs du Mal*, which he said had been left by another patient some time ago.

Well, when he produced the book, it was like a red rag to a bull. I started shouting and swearing – out of control. I told him what he could do with his gifts. It just struck me as terribly unfair that he could waltz in and out of my life, being bountiful or detached as he chose, and then just switch me off and go back to his real life, while I couldn't go anywhere. He was like God – and just as useless, I said. I hurled the book at the wall behind where he was sitting and stormed out. He didn't even get up.

Later, when I came back to my room after the obligatory post-lunch walk, I found the book of Baudelaire poems on my table. (One thing I'll say for Sigmund – he doesn't give up easily.) I ignored it for a while, but in the end I was so bored that I decided anything was better than sitting there doing nothing. So I sat down and spent the rest of the afternoon in the company of Baudelaire (fortunately, every poem was printed in both French and English).

There was one poem in particular which seemed to fit my mood just right. It was called *Un Voyage à Cythère*. Cythère is a wonderful isle situated supposedly somewhere near Crete and consecrated to love and the goddess Venus. The poem tells of the traveller's joy and anticipation on the voyage to Cythère – and his shock and horror when, on arriving at the island, he's met by the sight of a rotten corpse hanging from a gallows. It's a pretty grisly image. Not something you can get out of your mind easily. I couldn't, anyway. It even found its way into my dreams.

I don't very often remember my dreams at all. But this time I can recall them both very clearly. They were pretty weird – even Sigmund looked interested when I told them to him at our session today. And for him to look interested really is something.

* * *

Dream 1: I am walking along a very high rope bridge over a railway line with two people. They are dressed in strange clothes like a king and queen. I tell them that they ought to change before they go off on their journey. But they won't. Then I meet a tall man dressed in a black suit and I tell him that the woman is making the man go on a pointless journey. And then suddenly the scene changes and I am the traveller and I am going through customs. I open my suitcase and say calmly, 'See, there's nothing in it.' The customs officer seems to believe me. But then he roots further into the suitcase and finds something which I know is shocking – although I don't actually know what it is. I shrug my shoulders. 'Well, that's that, then,' I say.

Dream 2: Dad and I are walking through Paris and we come to a courtyard. In the courtyard there are lots of machines and foil. There are staircases too, going around the courtyard. Dad goes over and puts his foot on a staircase and I ask him what it all means. He gives me an explanation in French (which, I now realize, was utter gibberish). Then I ask him if I can take a sample of the foil. He says it's fine, but I look around, worried that someone might stop me. Then, all of a sudden, there is someone else in the courtyard – a woman. She is holding a noose. I feel worried, as though I know what is going to happen. When I look again, the woman has gone and the noose is round the neck of a rotting, bloody corpse hanging from a gallows.

While Madame Calimet made coffee I sat perched uneasily on the edge of her plush sofa, looking around at the smart opulence of her sitting room with its elegant vases, bright paintings, beautiful parquet floor and spotless sheepskin rugs. It was all very ordered and sort of clinically tasteful – very different from the haphazardness of home. I'd already caught sight of my unkempt, battered reflection in the huge gilt-edged mirror that adorned one wall and now, seeing myself again in the top of the glass coffee table, I felt even more like a fish out of water. My face was all whiskery with soft, long hairs – 'bum fluff' they called it at school; I needed a shave and a haircut. And my eye had come up a treat.

Now that I'd finally got where I'd wanted to be, the end of my journey, I wasn't quite sure what to do. I knew that I had to confront Madame Calimet, but she was the one who took control: as soon as she'd recovered from her amazement at hearing my name, her face had undergone a rapid transformation. Her frown had become a welcoming smile – like the one with which she'd met 'Merde' back at the stamp market. I knew it was phoney, but it was still difficult not to be overwhelmed. The next thing I knew I was being led into her apartment, invited to sit down and offered coffee. I'd hardly had a chance to say a word.

'I am very surprised to see you,' she said, with a smile, putting a tray with the coffee things on the table. She'd taken off the leather coat, and in a cream silk blouse and rust-coloured trousers she looked, well, not exactly warm, but less fierce somehow. She poured coffee into one of the two small white cups and offered it to me.

'Please serve yourself to sugar or milk,' she said. I took the cup.

'I suppose your father told you where I am living,' she said. Her smile was very seductive, enticing, flattering. Difficult to resist – except that I knew there was something quite different behind it. Seeing her close up, I noticed how heavily made-up she was: mascara, black eyeliner, brown eye shadow, rouged cheeks, thick lipstick, foundation . . . All of which made her look older in the flesh than she had in the photograph. More Mum's age. But Mum wore very little make-up. She didn't have to. She had what you'd call a natural beauty.

'No,' I said. 'Dad didn't tell me anything. I followed you

here from the stamp market. I was told you went there every Sunday.'

'Oh?' she queried. 'Who told you? A little bird?'

'Gerald Finch,' I said. 'One of his colleagues saw you and Dad there together.'

'Ah,' she said. 'Gerald.'

She took a sip of coffee and then put her cup down on the table. It clanked against the glass, like the bell ringing for the start of the second round.

She sat up in her chair and looked me in the eye.

'Well, *mon ami*,' she said, 'if you have been talking to Gerald, then I suppose you know what is what. We have no need to beat about the bush. I'm right? Gerald sent you?'

'No,' I said, 'Gerald didn't send me. I came because I wanted to. I came to find out who killed my mum and dad and why.'

'Ah, I see, and dear Gerald pointed the finger at me, umm? Madame Calimet, the wicked Frenchwoman.'

Then she said something in French, punctuating her words with a dismissive wave of her hand.

I didn't understand what she said, but I knew it was an insult – and it made my hackles rise in Gerald's defence.

'Gerald's all right,' I said. 'At least he's honest. He reckons that you were behind Mum and Dad's murder. But he didn't tell me to come. I'd already worked things

148

out for myself. It had to have something to do with you.'

Her reaction took me by surprise. I thought she'd be shocked or made furious by my implied accusation – but instead she threw up her hands and laughed. It was a shallow, rather ugly laugh, a little like Dad's when he was in one of his sarcastic moods. Her eyes had the same mocking expression as in the photograph.

'Ah,' she said, '*mon pauvre gosse*. Gerald did paint a black picture of me, didn't he? I am not surprised. We never did see eye to eye, Gerald and me. I do not think the French are his cup of tea . . . He is too English, the *salaud*. He was always jealous of the way that your father got on so well with the French people. Do not believe what Gerald says to you, *mon gamin*.' She paused for a moment, and pointed to her chest with one long, slim, purple-nailed finger. 'I did not kill your parents.'

It was a very impressive gesture, but its sincerity was undermined by the mockery that still lingered in her eyes. I got the feeling that the idea of truth meant no more to her than it does to a little kid: she'd say whatever would get her what she wanted and keep her out of trouble.

'That man you were talking to today at the market,' I said. 'He was the same man who burgled my parents' house, a couple of months after they were murdered. I know because I was there; I've still got the bruises from where he hit me. I know what he was looking for too –

and that he didn't find it. I know a lot of things . . . I know your name, where you live, that you work for the French competitor of UKA – I even know where your great-grandmother went to school. And that there was something between you and Dad. So don't treat me like a stupid kid – because I'm not.'

Her smile came back. But with a little more difficulty this time.

'You are a brave boy,' she said. 'You are like your father. You are not easily distracted . . . I am very sorry that you were hurt the other night. Jacques tells me you chased them like a lion. He did not mean to hurt you. Just stop you. But he had no choice. He is not a gentle man, is Jacques . . . Have some more coffee.'

I shook my head, but she filled my cup all the same. I was suddenly tired of her stalling. I wanted to know the truth. I had to try to provoke her into losing her control somehow.

'You had Dad killed because he was asking you for too much money for those UKA documents, didn't you?' I asked bluntly.

This time she made no attempt to smile. She slammed the glass coffee jug down on the table so hard that I was amazed it didn't break, and swore at me in French.

'You say I must not treat you like a stupid kid, but that is exactly how you behave,' she said vehemently, hands flying. 'You say you know everything, but you understand nothing . . . Your father and I were lovers. We were having an affair. He was going to come and live with me here in this apartment. If he would not have been murdered he would have been sitting there, where you are sitting now. And you and your mother would have been just memories. Do you really think I would have killed your father when I could have him and his papers the both?' She glared at me fiercely – and I glared back.

'I don't believe you,' I said. 'You're a liar. Dad wouldn't have left Mum for you. He wouldn't have.' I could hear the desperation in my voice.

'Oh, would he not?' she mocked. 'You will see.'

She stood up and stormed over to a bureau in a corner of the room. She opened one of the drawers and started searching in it frantically. Then she pulled something out – a letter. She flourished it angrily in front of me so that I could see the handwriting. My heart sank. I started to feel sick. I knew what was coming – even before she began reading out the letter to me. It was a love letter from Dad, dated just a couple of days before he died. And it confirmed what she'd told me. Her voice was triumphant as she read out Dad's words – passionate expressions of love, how he couldn't wait to be with her, to start his life over with her. And without us. He didn't say that – but he didn't need to. Dad wasn't just running out on his company and his country – he was running out on his family too. On Mum and me . . . I thought of those suitcases packed in the hall and I thought of poor Mum. Had she known about Dad? How must she have felt if she had? How could Dad have done that to her? To me? Tears started to burn my eyes. I put my hands over my ears and shouted at Madame Calimet to stop. It was horrible, torture – the kiss of Judas. Dad had betrayed us. Madame Calimet smiled – delighted no doubt at the evident distress she'd caused me.

'See,' she said smugly. 'I am not your killer. That *salaud*, Gerald, there is your killer. Why do you not accuse him? I wanted your father. I wanted those documents . . . I still want them. They are mine. That is why I sent Jacques to your house. I must have those documents. And you must help me get them. Your father wanted me to have them.'

'Sod your bloody documents,' I said. 'I don't care about your documents.'

'But I do, *mon gamin*,' she said. 'I do. And you must help me . . . Do not forget Jacques.'

She stood over me now, threatening. As she spoke, her hands thrust at me, like knives. Then she stood back, and her face relaxed a little. The mocking smile returned to her eyes.

'I will pay you, of course,' she said. 'I do not expect something for nothing.'

Her callousness shocked me much more than her threats had done. I stared at her, wondering how the hell Dad could have thought of leaving Mum – loving, warm, generous Mum – for this cold, mercenary, hard, painted bitch of a woman. And I hated him for it. I hated him with all my heart. Murdered or not, I hated him.

Madame Calimet carried on badgering me about the documents but I wasn't really listening any more. My head was full of Dad's betrayal. Suddenly, whether it was Gerald or Madame Calimet or some passing psychopath who was responsible for my parents' murder no longer seemed to matter. Nothing did. I felt empty, used up, discarded, like an old tin can tossed into the surf for people to throw stones at. Zombie-like, I unzipped my bag and took out the copy of *Thérèse Raquin*.

'Here, I think this is yours,' I said. 'Take it. I don't want it. I don't want anything of yours.'

She took the book from me.

'But this is the book,' she said, amazed. 'Where did you find it? This is *magnifique*.'

She opened the book and her eyes went straight away to the inside front cover. I'd stuck the sticker back as best I could, but it was still curling a bit at the edges. She ripped it off and plunged her fingers eagerly into the cotton-wool packing. It was obvious she knew what she

153

was looking for – but she didn't find it. Her fingers came out empty.

'Where is it?' she said, waving her hands at me again. 'What have you done with the film? Give me the film.'

'I haven't got it,' I said. 'I gave it to Gerald.'

This wasn't altogether a lie, because I'd decided at that moment that that was what I was going to do – as soon as I got back to England. It was the only right thing to do. The documents hadn't belonged to Dad and they certainly didn't belong to Madame Calimet – whatever she said. Giving the film back to Gerald might help to recompense him at least a little for the pain that Dad and I, between us, had caused him.

Madame Calimet wasn't going to give in easily though.

'I don't believe you,' she said. 'I am sure you have the film with you. Why do you not give it to me?'

I shrugged my shoulders.

'For your father . . .' she cooed flirtatiously.

It was the wrong thing to say. At that moment, just about the last person on Earth I'd have done anything for would have been Dad.

'Very well,' she said, 'if you will not play the game I have something to show you to change your mind. *Attend.*'

She got up from her chair and strode out of the room. Her heels tapped angrily across the wooden floor.

Leaning forward, I caught sight of my face again in the glass of the coffee table and I thought about Dad and wondered how many times he'd sat where I was sitting now, seeing his reflection in the glass. And I wondered just who it was he'd seen there. Not my dad, not Mum's husband, but some other man, a stranger to us. A sort of enemy . . . I was tired of this game of gambits and counter gambits. It seemed like I'd packed a whole lifetime into the past few days and I had no more energy or determination left. I'd run out of moves. I was beaten. I just wanted to leave.

I picked my bag up and walked quickly and quietly to the door and out into the hallway. From behind the closed door of a room opposite, I could hear the sound of Madame Calimet's voice. It sounded like she was talking to someone on the telephone. I held my breath and listened long enough to find out who it was she was talking to. Jacques! The name jolted my mind back into action. If she was calling Jacques, then I could be in big trouble. I shuddered at the memory of what he'd done to me before – and what he might do again if he had me trapped in Madame Calimet's apartment. It was time to get away, to abandon the game before I found myself in a very deadly checkmate.

I opened the front door and ran down the staircase, across the courtyard, through the entrance and out into the street. Then I carried on running, misery and self-preservation driving me on . . .

The next twenty-four hours are a blur of strange streets and bars, foreign voices, darkness . . . I don't think I slept and yet the whole time seems like a dream. A nightmare. I'd been abandoned . . .

Somehow, though, I did get home. Got on trains and a boat and ended up at Uncle Jim and Aunty Susan's, like a well-trained homing pigeon back to roost. Aunty Susan answered the door to me. She must have been in the middle of peeling the potatoes for supper, because she had a potato and a small knife in her hands. When I saw the knife I backed away. Aunty Susan said my name and she started crying. But I just kept staring at her hands. At the knife. I stood there, frozen, petrified. I was mesmerized by the knife and appalled at the idea that it was going to cut the potato. And then (here's one for your loony book, Sigmund) I *was* the potato and I felt the sharp blade cut into me. And I wouldn't move until Aunty Susan had put the knife down and given me the potato.

You could say, I suppose, that I've been like a potato faced with the knife ever since. All that changes is the face of the person holding the blade. Dad, Gerald, Jacques, Sigmund, Uncle Jim, Donnelly – even Lees and old Vanissart . . .

But most of all Madame Calimet. Her cold, hard, evil face haunts me. I hear her harsh voice, I see her treacherous smile, and I know that she's the one responsible for the death of Dad and Mum. My lovely, loving Mum. Yes, she's the guilty one.

Here's an irony – the pen I've been using to write all this down in the notebook for Sigmund is one Dad gave me. It's got UKA (FOIL) LTD printed on it in silver lettering. I suppose it's pretty appropriate really. Maybe Dad nicked that too. Anyway (symbolic or what?) now that I've finished my sorry tale the pen's stopped working. I was looking for another one today, in one of the drawers underneath the table – so that I could write down a few lines from Sigmund's Baudelaire book – when, lo and behold, what should I spy but Uncle Jim's letter – carefully smoothed out.

My first reaction was one of annoyance. I was getting a bit fed up of these sneaky gifts – first the book, now this. I grabbed the letter with the intention of tearing it up into the tiniest of tiny pieces so that no one could stick it or smooth it back together again – when a photograph fell out of the envelope. Like Madame Calimet's had that day when I'd found the copy of *Thérèse Raquin*. Only this wasn't a photo of Madame Calimet – it was a photo of a bride and bridegroom. I didn't recognize the happy couple, at first – and then I realized it was Mum and Dad.

I hadn't seen that particular photo before. I could hardly see it now, because my eyes misted over. Mum and Dad looked so young. Not all that much older than me. Mum looked beautiful in her white dress and so happy. She was laughing as Dad tried to hold back her veil, presumably so that the photographer could see her face. Dad was laughing too. They looked such a perfect, happy couple, with years of love and happiness before them. How could it all have ended as it had?

There were young men on either side of Mum and Dad. After careful scrutiny I realized that the one next to Mum, the slightly scruffy one in the shiny flared suit with the ridiculously large lapels, was Uncle Jim. Once I saw that, I couldn't tear up his letter. I took it out of the envelope and read it. It wasn't very long.

Dear Robert,
    How are you? Keeping your chin up, I hope. We know how difficult it's been for you. I'm sorry you don't feel that you can see me. But I do understand.
    Chief Inspector Donnelly came round yesterday. He says he's hopeful that his inquiries will soon

be over. He seems to think the gun could be the key. They've found it, you see. It was by chance, apparently. Somebody fished it up out of the river. He told me that the gun had always been the curious element in the case.

I've been feeling terrible, Robert, ever since our talk. The thing is, I don't know what to do. I feel as though I've really let you down over this whole business – and the last thing I want is for you to suffer more pain. So, if you feel you have to say something to Dr Ackfield, then don't hold back on my account. It's probably all up for me anyway. I've been thinking about making a clean breast of things to Chief Inspector Donnelly. Maybe if I have enough gin and tonics . . . The important thing is for you to get well. Dr Ackfield says you're definitely making progress and could be out for Christmas, which would really be wonderful. You deserve some good news after all you've been through. I'm proud of you, Robert. We all are. You really are very special and very brave.

I hope you like the photograph.

Aunty Susan sends her love and says she hopes to see you very soon. So, get better.

With sincerest best wishes and all my love,

your Uncle Jim

By the time I'd finished the letter there was no hint of tears in my eyes or in my heart. I was mad. And the more I've read the letter since, the madder I've got. There's something so bloody manipulative about it. He doesn't want me to say anything, but he's just too sneaky to come out and say it. He wants me to like him, but he doesn't want to make any bloody sacrifices. But what's really got me mad is the bit about Sigmund. Sigmund never tells me anything. He's certainly never suggested to me that I was taking any giant strides towards recovery (whatever that is) or even mentioned Christmas. Yet here he is chatting away to Uncle Jim about me behind my back . . . I, it seems, have no say in what happens to me – I'm not to be consulted. My life, my future, is in the hands of a conspiracy of adults from which I'm excluded . . . So they think.

I think otherwise. I've had more than enough of adults running and ruining my life. It isn't going to happen any more. Sigmund can go to hell. I'm going to get out of this place. But first, I'm going to find out just what Sigmund really does think about me. About my case. He's spent long enough prying into my thoughts; now I'm going to have a look at his. I want to know just what it is that he's been scribbling about me for the last couple of months, while I've sat there pouring out my soul. I know where to look – in his room – and I think I know how to get hold of the key.

I chose my time very carefully, because the timing was all-important. Between six and six-fifteen in the evening there was only one person in the office – a young guy called Vincent – and he was new. So that's when I decided to let off the fire alarm on my floor. They – Sigmund's crew – have a monitoring system which enables them to pinpoint just where an alarm's been activated. It saves them a hell of a lot of time, because in this place someone or other's always letting off the alarm. But – and this was significant – no one had done so since Vincent had started, which, I figured, would mean that he probably wouldn't be completely *au fait* with the procedure. I hoped so anyway, because my plan relied on his reaction to the alarm being a bit panicky.

At seven minutes past six I broke the glass and activated the alarm. Then I was off like a hare along the corridor, down the back stairs, wending my way to the office. It was a bit of a long route, but taking it meant that, if Vincent had done as I'd hoped and set off at once to investigate the source of the alarm, then I wouldn't meet him.

I didn't. The office door was ajar when I got to it and there was no one inside the room. I felt a buzz of exhilaration at the success of my plan. But I didn't have time to waste congratulating myself. It would only be a couple of minutes at most before Vincent or one of the others came in. But then a couple of minutes was all I needed.

I knew exactly where the keys would be – a great bunch of them hanging on a hook behind the desk. If I had to I'd take them all, but I would rather just take a little longer than I would have wanted – but after a desperate search through white plastic tab after white plastic tab, I eventually found it: *Dr Ackfield Room C17.* Getting it off the ring was much less of a problem than I'd thought it might be, but I didn't manage it a moment too soon, because no sooner was the key in my hand and free than the high-pitched tinkling came to an abrupt end. The alarm had been turned off.

The sudden quiet made me panic. I tried to move too quickly and slipped, knocking a coffee cup off the desk on to the floor. The noise of it smashing seemed about ten times as loud as the ringing of the alarm. For a moment I froze – like I'd frozen that night when I'd heard the burglars downstairs in the house. But there was still no sound of anyone in the corridor outside. I went quickly to the door, my heart thumping as though I was trying to get out of my body. There was no one in the corridor and I walked rapidly away.

I felt good. Really good. Very strong and capable. A couple of months before I'd never have had the guts to do what I'd just done. I felt like, well – I didn't actually think this then but looking back on it, this is how it was – I felt like the way I always thought Dad wanted me to be. He probably would have been prouder of me at that moment than he'd ever been, which is pretty ironic considering the way I was feeling about him . . .

Once I'd got the key, the rest was easy. I unlocked Sigmund's door and locked it again from the inside. I pulled down the small blind over the window in the door, then I clicked on the angle-poise lamp on his desk, bending it down low so that it wouldn't cast too much light. Then I started opening the drawers. When I got to the bottom one, I found a large leather-bound notebook with a black cover. I'd peeped through the door window and seen Sigmund writing in it once, when I'd been early for one of our sessions. It was a kind of journal. So this was it, I thought, the innermost reflections of Professor Sigmund. It wasn't actually what I'd come for – what I wanted were those bloody case notes that had to be around the place somewhere – but I thought it would be amusing to have a look at the journal anyway. Then I saw my name. And I started to read. And after a couple of entries I realized that this private journal was, basically, about me. So this *was* what I'd come for, after all. Not without some trepidation, I began once more to read . . .

Patient in a seriously traumatized condition following the shocking and brutal killing of his parents. 'Following' stress rather than 'due to'. The circumstance of the deaths themselves seems to be a catalyst for patient's state rather than the cause. Patient is articulate and lucid. He appears hostile rather than depressed. His hostility is directed against all adults and now, in particular, myself as adult/ doctor/figure of authority. Have asked him to relive rather than simply recall events in order to attempt to release him from strict regime of control he seems to have imposed on himself.

A very interesting and, I think, rewarding session. Robert was surprised when I asked him, not about his conscious feelings concerning his parents' deaths, but about a dream he had on his first night alone in the family house after the traumatizing event. He was very reluctant to offer me a serious interpretation of the dream – his resistance another example of his apparent desire to suppress any 'dangerous' material (but why 'dangerous'? And to whom?). Also, of course, an attempt to provoke me into a show of anger.

Robert's 'wild strawberry' dream on his first night back home provides some interesting family insights. It seems almost certain to me that Robert exercised some form of dream censorship on this particular element of his original narrative and attempted, consciously or subconsciously, to strengthen this in the analysis he then offered. Thus, he presents the 'wild strawberries' as a family joke, rather than as an indication of family and marital tension. His unease, he maintains, arises from a harmless natural anomaly (strawberries do not grow on trees) and not from the very real and disturbing anxiety about relationships within the family ('I am alone with my mother and having fun, but it will not last, because soon we must go to this other place with my father and my parents will argue – and I will be forced to take sides').

My impressions were confirmed by Robert's outraged reaction to my subsequent questioning on the subject of his parents and his own relationship with them. He became very defensive and abusive and seemed to feel

that I was accusing him of something. I believe, how-
ever, that in general these outbursts are not losses of
control but, on the contrary, attempts to exert control.
When pushed into a corner, Robert becomes abusive in
order to bring the session to an end on his terms.

There was a noise in the corridor. Voices. Footsteps. I turned out the light. And sat stone-still, listening, sweating a little. *Had they realized there was a key missing?*

The voices and footsteps went away down another corridor. I turned the light back on and returned to the book.

Decided that perhaps I had been a little too cool in my
treatment of Robert. He needs more encouragement.
Difficult while his attitude towards me is so hostile, but
the emotional needs implicit in his apparent negativity
very positive indeed and demand attention. He is
certainly responding. His narrative now is much more
immediate and 'objective' than at first. More honest. I
told Robert this in our session today. His response was,
though predictably negative, most interesting: a
convoluted warning about the veracity of his narrative
– which, though rather grudgingly offered, was offered
nonetheless. *He respects me enough not to want to lie*

to me. He is unable to come out and say what is really bothering him – he may not even be aware consciously of what it is – but he wishes me to catch him out.

Was keen to capitalize on this progress by questioning Robert further about his parents. So far, my feeling is that when Robert has been talking of his parents he has in fact been talking about his father. This kind of obsession is, of course, not at all unusual in young men of his age. It is his father whom he feels he has disappointed.

Robert's description of his mother was unequivocally flattering: elegant, open, decisive. But when I asked him for information of a more anecdotal but immediate nature, the incidents that came to mind pointed to a greater degree of ambivalence – in particular towards her decisiveness (or what might more accurately be termed 'impulsiveness'). This indicates to me that, in his feelings towards his mother, admiration and fear are two sides of the same coin: the same mother who rose heroically to fight for justice and her son's place in the football team was capable also, in a moment of anger, of taking and disposing of his favourite toys.

I believe this to have been a very important revelation, concluding a most encouraging session. PROGRESS at last.

* * *

Robert very disturbed today, voicing serious doubts about the efficacy of the treatment — eventually, inevitably turning to abuse. But against whom is this abuse really intended? His feelings towards his father appear to grow ever more hostile. Meanwhile his attitude towards his mother becomes increasingly 'romantic' — in his dreams she is a beautiful saintly vision.

I think that the strain of reliving the meeting with Gerald Finch, his father's colleague, was a very great one for Robert. The exchange, as he has described it, was both highly charged and emotionally draining — not only was Robert forced to confront the reality of his father's betrayal, with all the implications that contained, but also a certain violence within himself. Furthermore, the sight of a man whom he had formerly considered suave, manipulative, devious, strong, falling to pieces before his eyes undoubtedly had a profound and damaging effect both on Robert's view of adults and his relation to them, and, more fundamentally, on his faith in his own judgement. If he could be so wrong about Gerald, then might he not have been badly mistaken about his father too?

Talked with Jim Mowbray, Robert's uncle, today. He was

keen to see Robert, but Robert continues to refuse to receive any visitors. Do not think this is a bad thing. It is vital that Robert should continue to concentrate exclusively on reliving the events leading to his traumatization, especially as we have now, in my opinion, reached a critical stage. I explained this to Mr Mowbray, who was understanding, though reluctant to leave without attempting some sort of 'reconciliation' with Robert. He asked me to give Robert a note – despite my discouragement. As it turned out, however, I need not have worried, for Robert threw the note away without, I have since learned, even opening it.

I took the opportunity, while Mr Mowbray was in my office, of asking him a little more about the progress of the case. Little, it seems, has been made. I told him what Robert had told me of the morning he found his parents' objects in his uncle's loft – and Robert's version of the conversation that had afterwards taken place. He seemed rather taken aback – distressed even – for a moment or two. Obviously, he has still not reported the truth about the 'stolen' objects to the police. He confirmed Robert's story as true. It is clear from his attitude towards Robert and from what Robert has already said that there is a special bond between them.

I asked him a couple of questions about his late sister and brother-in-law and how he saw their relationship. He was very positive about this, declaring that they were a perfectly matched couple and very happy. I did not tell him of the very different impression I had been given, albeit reluctantly, by Robert himself. I believe that the treatment has clearly established that fairly intense family tensions did exist and were openly expressed. Mr Mowbray strikes me as an intelligent and by no means insensitive man — why, then, make a statement which is so palpably untrue? Is he protecting family honour? Perhaps, but somehow he does not seem the type. What then? Could it be himself? Or Robert even?

I felt hot and agitated all of a sudden and my face was burning. The lamp seemed to be giving off an intense heat – but I knew it wasn't. It was what was written in that damn book that was the cause. What was written about me – and Uncle Jim. I got up from the desk and went over to the window. The black roller blind was down. I put my head underneath it, unscrewed the window catch and pulled up the sash. It was virtually pitch-black outside, apart from the yellow lights of the town and a few stars. The air that came into the room was cold and frosty and make me shiver almost at once. It was wonderfully refreshing, though. But then I suddenly thought about the lamp and that someone might see its light and see me at the window, so I pulled the window down again, just leaving it a little bit open, and ducked back underneath the blind. I sat down and started to read once more. I could hardly bear to – and yet at the same time I knew I had to . . .

Robert's narrative appears to be approaching its climax. His journey to Paris is now more than a quest, it has become a rite of passage; he has inadvertently discovered conclusive proof of his father's guilt, he feels shame at his treatment of his father's colleague, he feels called to avenge the murder of his innocent mother, and he is on the verge of what he certainly believes will be a highly significant and conclusive confrontation with Madame Calimet.

In my opinion, however, of greater interest and encouragement is the concomitant 'sub-narrative', composed of the various comments (often of a rhetorical nature) with which Robert glosses his story. I found one – in today's instalment – most intriguing and, I must confess, gratifying too, as it related to the speculations I made following the last session. Walking down the platform to catch the train, Robert turned to see his uncle standing at the barrier, watching him 'with a look of real concern'. Robert then, in passing, makes the comment that he felt guilty 'because I was still naive enough to think he was concerned about me'. It is a quite extraordinary statement to make – accusatory, and yet there is no hint of explanation offered. It is, of course, always possible that Robert is simply projecting his current hostility on to his account of past events – but I do not think such an inter-pretation is consistent with his method of narration since the difficult early days of the treatment. Which leads me to deduce that something that happened or was said subsequently made it plain to Robert that his uncle's expression was not of concern for his nephew, but . . . But what? But an expression of worry – fed by guilt – that Robert might discover something that would implicate him in the murders?

I have spent the past hour with Robert's notebook in front of me, re-examining his narrative, and am now convinced that Robert's uncle is implicated in some way in the killing of Robert's parents and that Robert is aware of this. My conviction is based on three important pieces of evidence. The first comes early on in the narrative – a slip of the pen which I ought to have picked up on at the time. In his commentary on his initial questioning by the police, Robert praises the support he received from his uncle, concluding with the statement 'God knows what would have happened if he hadn't been around'. After this, he begins a new sentence with the words 'But then' – but decides not to continue and crosses the words out. Why? Could it be to protect his uncle? And perhaps the completed sentence would have gone something like, 'But then none of this would have happened if it hadn't been for him'? The other pieces of evidence, I believe, support this conclusion.

After the second break-in, Robert's uncle seems to take it for granted that this incident and the earlier one are not connected (as if somehow he knew this to be the case – which, indeed, he did). Then, later, when Robert reveals what Donnelly had said about his father having a gun, Mowbray appears, according to Robert's account, to be more worried than when threatened with the air pistol. This anxiety appears to ease when Mowbray learns that the gun has not been found.

It is now almost midnight and I have returned to my room to consult my case file on Robert Harrison. I haven't been able to get it out of my mind all evening. Which meant, unfortunately, that I took in little of tonight's production of King Lear. Indeed, I found my *thoughts turning to that other great 'family' tragedy, Hamlet. A play of two brothers, one woman and a son . . . A very similar grouping of characters to those in Robert's narrative. Only, in this case, the second brother is brother to the woman not the man. But is he also the villain?*

I asked myself these three questions: does it seem probable, given the facts and also my own first-hand impressions of Robert's uncle, that Jim Mowbray would murder his sister and her husband; and then, supposing this to be the secret knowledge, the 'taboo' that undoubtedly exists between Robert and his uncle, would it account for Robert's neurosis and his hostile attitude towards adults? Finally, would Robert's behaviour in general be consistent with this conclusion? I am an analyst, not a detective, of course, but my answer to all three questions would be 'no'. The key, I decided, is Robert's attitude towards his mother, which in the course of his narrative has become progressively more adoring – reverential even. In my opinion, therefore, it is not feasible that Robert would protect his mother's killer from the justice which it has been his whole aim to procure. Except in one instance. And one instance alone.

I turned the page. And the next. My fingers were clammy

with sweat. I felt feverish. I didn't want to read any more about *Hamlet* or *King Lear* – or any other family tragedy come to that. Not even my own. I just wanted to get to the end. I started reading again.

> *A difficult, volatile session. I had thought that Robert's attitude towards me was improving. But I had mis-judged the strength of Robert's resentment of his father. Consequently, my offer of a volume of Baudelaire's poetry (evidently a favourite with his father) was met by a paroxysm of rage and abuse. Robert is still unable, it seems, to make a real distinction between his feelings towards me and his feelings towards his father. I have arranged for the book to be put in his room. Perhaps if I am not actually seen to be giving it, the gift will seem more accept-able.*

> *A red-letter day. Robert recounted two dreams he had last night. My interpretation of them leads me to believe that, beyond almost any doubt, I know the true conclusion to Robert's narrative – although I doubt whether Robert is yet ready to reach it himself . . .*

Dreams, beliefs, conjecture . . . I wanted to get to the end. I wanted to know where it all led. The proof. I was tired of all this theorizing. I turned the page again, impatiently – and again, until I came to the final entry, dated the day before. I skipped through the first couple of paragraphs of preamble and began reading properly about halfway through.

After the admirable detail of his account, Robert's conclusion is unusually elliptical. Robert concludes his narrative by pointing the finger, in a rather weary and half-hearted fashion, at Madame Calimet, despite her protestations of innocence and a lack of any real evidence – but in accordance with his own urgent desire not to face the distressing alternatives. He cannot come out openly and reveal the killer's identity – all must be ambiguous. But now, it seems, the red herrings are at an end. In the light of my interpretation of his dreams, the final sentences of his narrative can have only one reading. Robert's grammatical construction is strikingly precise. There is no ambiguity.

The problem remains, however, of making Robert consciously face and accept the true cause of his distress. Now that he has reached the end, if not the conclusion, of his narrative, I feel that it is time to encourage a little outside contact. I have, therefore, arranged for the letter from Robert's uncle to be placed in his room, in the hope that Robert in a calmer mood may read it (I am encouraged by his response to my 'gift' of the Baudelaire volume). The next few days will, I'm sure, be crucial.

I read this entry a couple of times, my heart beating fast. Someone went by, pushing a trolley down the corridor. There was a metallic rattling as it passed. But I wasn't really scared any more about being discovered. It might even be a relief. Because I'd got to the end without learning anything too terrible. Sigmund reckoned he'd rumbled me, but he hadn't proved it yet. Not to me anyway.

I put my elbows on the table and sat with my head in my hands. The tension of the last hour or so (I had no idea just how long it had been since I'd left my room) had really kept me buzzing – but now I felt drained. I wanted to close my eyes and sleep but there was far too much on my mind for me to be able to do that.

The longer I sat, the more relief turned to disappointment. The sort of feeling you get when you take a thriller out of the library and read it to the end, only to discover the all-important last page is missing. Sigmund thought he knew the solution – and I had to know too. It was just a question of whether I dared turn back the page and find out. Back to the dreams. I could just close the book now, put it back in the drawer, turn off the lamp and walk out

– and no one would be any the wiser. I'd have stolen a march on Sigmund and that's really all I'd wanted to do. I could keep this resistance up for ages, I thought.

Yes, I could . . . But that wouldn't solve anything, though, really, would it? Not in the end. Because in the end I'd have to co-operate or stay in this place for ever. For ever. Until I was dead too – like Mum and Dad. But then I'd really go mad, wouldn't I? And I didn't want to be mad. I just wanted it all to be over. Finished . . . I wanted to bury my dead.

I took a deep breath. Then, with trembling fingers, I turned back the page and found the entry I'd given up reading before . . .

A red-letter day. Robert recounted two dreams he had last night. My interpretation of them leads me to believe that, beyond almost any doubt, I know the true conclusion to Robert's narrative – although I doubt whether Robert is yet ready to reach it himself.

Of the two dreams, the first is particularly significant. The second is more straightforward (although more complex than it appears) in that it reflects the manifest concerns and elements of Robert's narrative and existence at present: his father, Paris, the courtyard through which he pursued Madame Calimet, the foil which has been the material cause of all his

trouble and Robert's anxiety about it and distrust of his
father – and, of course, the macabre corpse from the
Baudelaire poem which he found so striking.

Robert identifies himself with the poet or narrator of
the poem in his quest for an idealized world (just as he
identified himself with the drawing-room geography
students in the Longhi painting) and his subsequent
disillusion. It is typical, however, of Robert's tendency
towards half-truths and distortions that he stops short
of making a comparison, as does the poet, between the
corpse and himself. In the dream, therefore, the corpse
is simply that of his father and reflects Robert's bloody
experience of death. The murderer is a woman – presumably Madame Calimet . . . And yet where in all this
is his mother? What if the corpse were indeed as much
the image of himself as his father?

The first dream, I believe, establishes the crucial
relevance of these questions. The dream is in two
distinct parts, both concerning travelling, which
physically and metaphorically have preoccupied
Robert during the last months – and, as Robert himself
is aware, journeys in dreams are often symbolic of
death ('the undiscovered country from whose bourn no
traveller returns' as Hamlet has it – and, one might
add, where wild strawberries grow on trees).

In the second part of the dream Robert himself is the

traveller, having to go through customs – just as he did in his narrative. In his dream, however, he has no worries about the outcome. He opens his suitcase and announces calmly that there is nothing in it. And the customs officer seems to believe him. The 'seems' is all-important. Because the officer continues searching and does indeed find something which to Robert is shocking – although he does not know why.

It requires no great feat of analysis to deduce that I am the customs officer. The suitcase which Robert has opened with such apparent confidence is his own narrative, which has indeed been largely matter-of-fact – something for which I have encouraged and, on occasions, praised him; thus 'seeming', at least, to believe him. What follows is an exhortation to me to continue searching (as was his earlier caution that his account might not be altogether honest) and so find the 'shocking' thing which is at the root of his distress and which, in a conscious state, he has tried so hard to avoid uncovering. 'Well, that's that, then,' he says with a shrug, handing me the initiative – and the key, which I am sure is to be found in the vital first part of the dream.

Robert's anxiety is plain from the precarious situation he and his two companions find themselves in – walking on a rope bridge high above a railway line.

The identity of the companions is clear enough too –
'king and queen' are fairly common dream symbols for
mother and father. It is also quite usual, after the loss
of loved ones, to experience dreams in which there is a
curious compromise between knowledge of death and
the desire to bring the person – or in this case
persons – back to life again. Only if they know themselves to be *dead will they* be *completely dead.* In his
dream, Robert worries that the strangeness of his
parents' attire will make it clear to them, when they
arrive at their destination, that they are indeed dead.
Thus his attempt – but failure – to make them change.
The tall man in the black suit is undoubtedly death
itself, quite possibly in the guise of Chief Inspector
Donnelly, whom Robert associates with the murder of
his parents.

But the key – the key for which I have been searching these past weeks – is, I feel certain, in the words
that follow:

'I tell him that the woman is making the man go on
a pointless journey.'

Robert's mother made his father go on a pointless
journey. According to Robert, therefore, his father's
death was 'pointless'. The sort of definite, conclusive
statement that could only really be made by someone
in possession of all the facts. But then Robert knows the

facts – he has all along. This is the terrible knowledge that is the cause of Robert's traumatized state – not the deaths themselves. And, poor lad, is it any wonder he's in the state he's in? He knows what I had begun to suspect: that it was his mother who killed his father – and then turned the gun on herself.

There was more, but I didn't read it. How could I with my eyes tight shut and, anyway, so full of tears? I sobbed, I cried, I wept, my whole body shaking, my fists tightly clenched against my temples, then thumping down hard on the desk, pummelling the wood like they pummelled the coffin lids that day at the funeral, begging to be admitted. But now they were blows of protest, of rage.

I didn't see the door open. Looked up only when I heard his voice. Then I stood up and I shouted. I can't remember exactly what I said, but it wasn't pleasant. Four-letter word after four-letter word, abuse, accusations . . . He was a bastard and a bloody hypocrite; always burdened me with his disappointment then let me down; abandoned me; rejected my love; never there when I needed him; two-faced; betrayer; ruined Mum's life; destroyed mine.

'I hate you!' I shouted.

'I hate you!' I cried.

'I HATE YOU!' I screamed at the top of my voice.

And then he said my name again, softly, almost tenderly. And in that moment I understood that the man standing there in the doorway wasn't Dad. It was the man who'd been sitting opposite me, behind this desk where I was now standing, for all those days, all those weeks. The man who'd been trying to help me. It was Sigmund – Dr Ackfield – not Dad. Dad was dead and buried (I'd been at the funeral – that bloody, heartbreaking funeral). And so was Mum.

And thinking of Mum I understood something else too. Something it wasn't nice to know (but, well, when you know something, you know something and, however terrible, however horrible, it doesn't change the fact that you know it) – I knew that when I'd screamed *I hate you*, I hadn't just meant Dad, I'd meant Mum too. In fact it was Mum I really hated most. Dad had pulled things apart, but it was Mum who'd destroyed them. It was Mum who'd done the killing. Mum who'd made me an orphan . . . Mum.

And how the hell could I ever forgive her?

So here it is then – finally – the end of the story, the true end of the story. The bit about the potato and the knife – that was true enough. But there was more. A lot more. Standing there on the doorstep, I was ranting, talking gibberish. When I finally crossed the threshold into the house, Uncle Jim tried to calm me down. Aunty Susan was crying. I kept on about Madame Calimet and Jacques. How they had to be caught and punished. Justice had to be done. I wanted Uncle Jim to phone Donnelly right away and tell him that I'd found the murderers. When he tried to persuade me to wait until I was in a calmer state, I said I'd ring Donnelly myself. I went to pick up the phone and he moved to stop me. We started tussling. I must have tripped over something because I ended up on the floor – with the receiver in my hand. I pressed out 999 and waited for the ringing tone.

Uncle Jim was standing over me. He said, 'For God's sake, Robert, put the bloody phone down.

185

Please. That French woman didn't kill your mum and dad.'

I looked across at him, puzzled.

'How do you know?' I asked.

There was a click and a woman's voice came on the line.

'Because,' said Uncle Jim, and he closed his eyes and grimaced.

'Which service, please?' the woman's voice asked, mechanically, from a long long way away.

'Because,' he repeated, 'I know who did.'

By the time I left the house that morning to go to school – after Mum and I had heard that broadcast about exam results and geography – Dad had been gone for a couple of hours. Off to work, we both presumed. But he didn't go to work. He couldn't go to work because they'd soon rumble he'd taken the project papers – and anyway, he'd already planned to do a bunk and go off to France. He probably spent the morning finalizing his travel arrangements. Then, when he knew Mum would have left for work, he went back to the house and packed. Then he phoned Mum at Aunty Barbara's shop and asked her to meet him there. At least he had the decency to face her before he left – he didn't just slink off without a word. But, as it turned out, that was his fatal mistake.

When she arrived at the house, I suppose he was all

ready to go. He probably told her about the papers and about Madame Calimet, that he was leaving – and knowing Mum, she probably had a fit. Went crazy. And no doubt Dad provoked her with a few well-chosen words of sarcasm, a few twisted home truths. Pushed her too far. So she got the gun (the one he'd bought because of the warnings or threats he'd had from those government people – whoever they were; the one he'd bought, ironically, to protect himself) – like she'd got the big black bag that time and taken away all of my toys. And he probably egged her on, tried to humiliate her, thinking she'd never have the nerve to use the gun . . . And, finally, she shot him. And that was that. The end of Dad.

She was pretty hysterical when she phoned Uncle Jim and he could hardly make out what she was saying.

'He's gone. David's gone,' she kept repeating.

He thought that Dad had left her and tried to calm her down. He said something about Dad coming back.

'No,' she said. 'He can't come back. Don't you understand? I've killed him.'

By the time he got to the house, Mum had shot herself. There was blood everywhere – like it was in the newspaper photograph. He says it was horrible, shocking – he ran outside again and threw up. For a while, he stayed there, retching and gasping, unable to think about anything. Then, after a bit, he thought about phoning the

187

police. He went inside to do it, started dialling, then stopped.

He didn't phone the police at that moment because, he said, he suddenly thought about me and the effect this terrible scene would have on me. How dreadful it would be for me to know that my mother had murdered my father and then killed herself. There was no way, of course, that I could be spared the grief of Mum and Dad's death – but I could be spared the knowledge that it was self-inflicted. And that's when he started to think about making it look like a robbery that had gone tragically wrong. He messed the place up a bit more to make it look like a burglary, he collected up what he thought were the most valuable items – only, not being an expert, he left the bird jug – and he took the gun. He even cleaned the black specks of cordite off Mum's hand, so that no one would know she'd pulled the trigger. With the gun gone, he thought, there could be no question of Mum's death being considered suicide. Then he drove off. He was taking a bit of a chance, because someone could have seen him – but there are only a few houses in the cul-de-sac and there didn't seem to be anyone around, so he thought he was safe. (He was right.) He phoned the police from a call box. Then he drove to a quiet part of the river and threw the gun in. He should have got rid of the other stuff too, but he said he couldn't, because they'd been some of Mum's favourite things. So he went home and hid the vase, the thimbles, the chess set and the pottery figures in his attic. He didn't think there was any reason why they should be found there. What he didn't bargain for, though, was that I'd go poking around up there looking for his air gun.

This then was the 'secret knowledge' that Dr Ackfield had correctly suspected lay between Uncle Jim and me. My bloody family saga. The knowledge that I'd tried to suppress in my narrative. I had to for Uncle Jim's sake. If the police found out, then he'd be ruined – he'd go to prison, he'd said. I didn't want to be responsible for that. Like they say, blood is thicker than water – and I'd seen enough of it spilt already to last me several lifetimes. I didn't want to lose any more.

I've just been reading my last piece back and I'm struck by how calm and matter-of-fact it sounds. Like the person talking wasn't me at all, but a sort of objective narrator. Very different from how it all came out that night in Dr Ackfield's office, when I first told him the whole story. When I admitted that all those saintly visions of Mum I'd described were just a sham, an invention, an evasion – whatever you will. The image I'd had of Mum, ever since I'd seen that newspaper photo, had been of a bloody, half-smashed face. A monster. But recalling that image made me think of her 'guilt', that she'd been the killer, so I described another image entirely – one that was beautiful, saintly, innocent. The Mum I'd loved. The Mum in the wedding photo. The Mum who's gone for ever . . .

A week's gone by now, since that night of discovery. And in that week it feels like we've covered more ground than we did in the whole of the months before. I feel like a different person. A great weight's been lifted off me. I've been able to talk freely about Mum and Dad without feeling I'm betraying anyone. It hasn't been easy – there have been lots of tears and heartache, but there's been a lot of relief too. The violence and aggression have gone. Only the sadness and loss remain. Maybe, some day, I'll even be able to forgive them all, totally, for the lies they told, the lies they lived – and feel that I'm forgiven too, for having been such a disappointment. I hope so.

I had a letter from Uncle Jim this morning. He says that he thinks he should put the house on the market soon – to help pay the various expenses that have arisen from my parents' death (my time in this place, for a start) and to make sure I'm well provided for. He wants me to go and stay with him and Aunty Susan. Not just for Christmas, but permanently.

But, well, that's not what I want. It's not that I really mind about his selling the house – I couldn't go back there now anyway. It's more that I don't feel the same way about Uncle Jim any more, since what happened, and the part he played in it. It's not that I hold a grudge, it's just that I feel differently towards him. I couldn't go and live in his house, because he'd want to treat me like his son and I'm not his son. I'm not anyone's son. I'm my own father and my own mother now. And also, if I'm honest, I don't think I really respect Uncle Jim any more – and that saddens me.

In his letter he says he's sure it's only a matter of time

before Donnelly cracks the case and that maybe he should make a clean breast of it before he does. But 'maybe' isn't good enough really. And the reason, I suspect, that he won't confess is the same reason he tried to cover up in the first place – not for my sake, but to protect his own interests. I don't think I came into his considerations much when he stood there over Mum and Dad's dead and bloody bodies – what came into his mind, I think, was the awful effect on his political career that the scandal of a 'murderer' sister would have; the disapproving faces down at the golf club. By contrast, the huge public sympathy he'd gain from having a sister and brother-in-law who were the victims of murder would see him ensconced in the mayor's office in no time. I'm not saying he didn't feel any grief about Mum and Dad. It's just that he couldn't help trying to turn things to his advantage. I guess he's just too much of a politician.

Today is December the twenty-third. Dr Ackfield has warned me that Christmas is going to be a difficult time – that I'll probably relapse a bit. I had three Christmas cards today – one from Aunty Barbara, one from Gerald Finch, thanking me for returning the microfilm and apologizing for what had happened (*he* was apologizing to *me*!) and one from my class at school: Garth, Lucy, Caroline, Bozo . . . They'd all signed it. Even old Lees had written something. Getting that completely overwhelmed me. I cried a little, but the tears that came were sort of gentle, I could almost say pleasurable. I'm actually pretty tearful, generally, at the moment, which isn't like me. Dr Ackfield says it's a good sign. That I'm facing up to my grief. Not evading it – like I was doing, I suppose, with all those tantrums and antics, which, I have to admit, seem pretty childish when I look back on them: calling Dr Ackfield 'Sigmund' and all that. He says, though, that the sort of negative reaction I expressed (transferring all my feelings of anger on to him instead of Dad and Mum) can often be positive in the end. It doesn't stop me feeling pretty embarrassed about my behaviour, though, even so. And I still feel embarrassed when I think about the way I acted at the funeral.

Throughout the service I'd felt like I was being torn apart. But I didn't cry, though everyone around me did. But when we got to the graveside and they lowered the coffins into the open grave, I just cracked completely. I threw myself in after them, clinging to the coffins, hammering on the lids, begging to be admitted, shouting to them all to bury me too. It took about four men to pull me out, whimpering and swearing. I suppose I must have upset quite a few people.

We talked a bit about that today. We also talked about Uncle Jim and what I'd written about him. Dr Ackfield wondered if I wasn't being too harsh on him. I said I didn't think so, because at long last I knew all the facts, so that I could make a fair judgement. Dr Ackfield smiled when I said that. He doesn't smile very often, but when he does I always find it a bit of a shock because he suddenly becomes a human being, a person, rather than the listening machine he usually seems.

'All the facts, Robert?' he queried. 'Surely you'd have to be a god to know all the facts.'

'I thought that men of science didn't believe in God,' I said.

'I'm not sure that we do,' he said.

He's not exactly committal, is Sigmund.

'I want to show you something,' he said.

He went over to his bookshelves and came back with a large book. It was a book of Italian paintings.

'I was looking through this book,' he said, 'and I came across the painting by Pietro Longhi that you so admire.'

'*The Geography Lesson*,' I said.

'Yes, *The Geography Lesson*.'

He opened the book at a certain page and looked at it for a moment.

'*La Lezione di Geografia*,' he read. Then he looked at me with that ultra-calm expression I've grown so used to and that once annoyed me.

'Would you say, Robert, that this is something you know completely?'

I smiled. 'Better than anything else in the world,' I said.

Dr Ackfield smiled too. 'I thought so,' he said. 'You'd know then, for instance, exactly how many figures there are in the painting.'

'Yes,' I said. 'Four.'

'I see,' he said and turned the book round so that the painting was facing me. 'Now, have a careful look at this.'

It had been a while since I'd seen the painting – having been accustomed to seeing it just about every day of my life – and it was with warm pleasure that I looked at it now. It was like meeting a friend in a strange place. There were the three elegant figures: the woman with the globe on the table in front of her; the main in blue, probably her tutor, who stood over her, with a sort of eyeglass in his hand; and the portly, rather florid man in brown, who sat by the bookcase, an atlas in his hands and another splayed open at his feet. And there was the young maid, standing, waiting, with a tray of tiny cups. But – and this was the shock – there was someone else in the picture too. Someone I'd never seen before, because in our print she hadn't been there. She was an elderly woman, another maid probably, standing behind the younger servant, who, in our print at home, had been at the very edge of the painting. The elderly woman was only half visible in the gloom but the point was, she was there. And there was something rather eerie about her – only half there, her face looming out of the darkness, worried, fore-boding . . . It changed the whole tone of the painting. It put something of a dampener on the very positive spirit of adventure that had always seemed to me to flood out from that geography student and her tutors. I was no longer sure just what I felt about what I was seeing.

I'm still not sure now, sitting here, on the end of my

bed, with the book open before me (Dr Ackfield let me borrow it – he seems to have become my librarian as well as my shrink). One thing is for sure, though – Sigmund (I mean Dr Ackfield) certainly made his point. No one can know everything. Maybe I have been too hard on Uncle Jim, maybe he really did do what he did for me and not just for his own ends. I know he cares about me. I just need time to work things out, that's all.

The sky is really beautiful this evening. I've been watching it for the past hour as it's turned from a very clear and unblemished blue, with violet and grey patches down near the skyline, to a wonderfully crisp royal blue. Now the stars are out too. If only everything could be this simple, this lovely. If only things had turned out differently that day. If Dad had just gone away without confronting Mum. It's silly to wish it, I know, but I can't help it. I can't help thinking back to this time last year either – Christmas – and what we were all doing. It seems like we were having a really good time, being a family – Mum, Dad, me and Uncle Jim and Aunty Susan. I know Christmas is one of those times that nearly always seems better in retrospect, but it's nice to be *able* to look back at it with pleasure even so. I can't any more. Which is why I've decided to forget Christmas this year. It's a time for families, and I no longer have one. Gerald and Gordon can have my Christmas. I'll stay here and try and pick up the pieces of my life.

I played a game of chess yesterday. My first for ages. I felt pretty rusty, but I really enjoyed it. While I was playing, my mind cleared of everything except the game, my next move. My opponent was Vincent, the young student auxiliary. He's not a bad player. I beat him, but it was a close contest. We're going to start another game later. He says he knows of another guy here – a patient – who plays, so he's going to try and set up a kind of mini-tournament over Christmas, which, hopefully, might help me not to brood on things so much.

I have to try and stop brooding so much. To try and live in the present – that's what Dr Ackfield says. The past is just too painful – it's Mum and Dad, what I haven't got; it's like a chess game that someone came along and ruined by smashing all the pieces off the board. And the future's no better. Thinking about it scares and depresses me. It's like a long, long emptiness that somehow I've got to fill. God knows how, or with what . . . Maybe old Donnelly wasn't so off the mark with his hoping, after all. Life can be a pretty desperate business – death too. Perhaps all you can do is hope.

I'm not going to write in the notebook any more. It was useful before, but now . . . well, the story's finished and, anyway, everything seems much worse when you write it down and then have it staring you in the face. It's like everything I've written so far's been written in blood, not ink. Bloodlines. Bloodstains. Not the kind you can wash out with washing powder, but the kind that linger for ever. It's not that I want them to go away; I just don't want to have to look at them every minute of every day for the rest of my life, that's all. So I've decided that from now on the notebook is strictly for the recording of chess results and strategy only.

I wonder what Dr Ackfield will make of that.